THE BACKYARD SECRETS OF DANNY WEXLER

THE BACKYARD SECRETS

OF DANNY WEXLER

KAREN POKRAS

KAR-BEN PUBLISHING

KAR-BEN PUBLISHING®
An imprint of Lerner Publishing Group, Inc.
241 First Avenue North
Minneapolis, MN 55401 USA

Website address: www.karben.com

Cover illustration by Zhen Liu.
Additional background texture by Yurlick/Shutterstock.com.

Main body text set in Bembo Std.
Typeface provided by Monotype Typography.

Library of Congress Cataloging-in-Publication Data

Names: Pokras, Karen, author.
Title: The backyard secrets of Danny Wexler / Karen Pokras.
Description: Minneapolis : Kar-Ben Publishing, [2021] | Includes bibliographical references and index. | Audience: Ages 9–13. | Audience: Grades 4–6. | Summary: "Eleven-year-old Danny Wexler, the only Jewish boy in his blue-collar town during the late 1970s, investigates a local kid's disappearance, a possible UFO invasion, and the Bermuda Triangle, all while dealing with his community's anti-Semitism" —Provided by publisher.
Identifiers: LCCN 2020035827 (print) | LCCN 2020035828 (ebook) | ISBN 9781728412948 | ISBN 9781728412955 (paperback) | ISBN 9781728428901 (ebook)
Subjects: CYAC: Family life—Fiction. | Schools—Fiction. | Jews—United States—Fiction. | Antisemitism—Fiction. | Bullying—Fiction.
Classification: LCC PZ7.1.P6416 Bac 2021 (print) | LCC PZ7.1.P6416 (ebook) | DDC [Fic]—dc23

LC record available at https://lccn.loc.gov/2020035827
LC ebook record available at https://lccn.loc.gov/2020035828

Manufactured in the United States of America
1-48539-49041-2/12/2021

TO MY CHILDREN, WHO INSPIRE ME
WITH EVERY QUESTION AND DREAM

CHAPTER 1
HAIRY MYSTERY

My older sister, Alice, told me my new piano teacher, Mr. Schneider, was part tarantula. At first, I didn't believe her, but lately, I wasn't so sure. Even his name rhymed with spider.

Mr. Schneider's fingers were long, pointy, and covered in a million tiny black hairs. More hairs than I'd ever seen on anyone's hands before. I couldn't stop staring at them. They scurried across the piano as he played, leaving a trail of sweaty prints.

"Daniel?" Mr. Schneider asked.

My attention snapped up to his head. He was completely bald. Did tarantulas have bald spots? And why would Mr. Schneider have so much hair in one place but none up top?

"Daniel!" His voice echoed off of the walls in my living room.

"Sorry." I put my fingers on the keys, careful to avoid his sweat marks. Nothing I played sounded right.

My tarantula teacher sighed. "Our time is up. One hour of practice every day. Got it?"

"Yes, sir."

He stood, but didn't move.

"So, see you next week?" I took two steps toward the front door hoping Mr. Hairy-hands would get the hint it was time for him to leave. He still didn't budge.

"Did your mother leave anything for me?" He remained standing next to our piano.

"Right." My body stayed straight and confident while I walked backwards to get to the entry table where Mom had left his check. I kept my eyes on him the entire time. I learned that in science class. Out in the wild, a predator was more likely to pounce the moment its prey turned its back. My living room wasn't exactly the wild, but tarantulas were poisonous. And the longer we stood there, the more Mr. Schneider's eyes bulged. I wasn't taking any chances.

"Here you go." I held his weekly payment by the

edge of the corner, making sure our fingers didn't touch when he snatched it from me.

"Thank you." He shoved the envelope into his shirt pocket. "I'll see you next week, Daniel. And don't forget to practice." He darted out the door and scuttled away.

I sat back down at the piano. An hour of practice started with fifteen minutes of scales, the most boring thing ever—even more boring than math homework, if you can believe that.

Mom's 1976 collector's plate sat on top of the piano. It rattled in its stand as I played. Mom had a thing about dishes, and we had more than anyone else I knew. We had everyday eating ones, fancy china for holidays and company, and Mom's even fancier collector plates that no one was allowed to touch, ever . . . not even Dad. Most of those were kept in the glass cabinet in the dining room, but Mom liked to keep this 1976 one on top of the old piano that used to be in Grandma Esther's house. Grandma gave us the piano last year when she moved into the nursing home in Larston. That's when I started taking lessons.

Mom got this 1976 plate two years ago at the bicentennial celebration. July 4, 1976, was a big deal.

Here in Croyfield we had a huge parade with marching bands and people dressed up as old-fashioned soldiers. Afterward, we all went down to the river to watch the big ships roll by. Even our neighbor, old Mrs. Albertini, came out to see the fireworks, and she hardly ever left her house.

"Enough with that racket!" Alice stood in the doorway of the living room with her hands on her hips. She was fifteen years old and thought she was the boss of me, especially when Mom and Dad weren't home.

"I'm supposed to practice," I told her. "An hour a day. Mr. Schneider just said so."

"He didn't mean starting today. You just had a lesson. That *was* your hour, dork face."

"You're a dork face," I said.

"Good one." She rolled her eyes. "It's five-thirty. Dad's going to be home soon."

I followed her into the kitchen. Friday was the day Mom worked late at the hospital. Well, Wednesdays and Fridays. Those were the days Alice and I had extra chores.

"What's for dinner?" I asked.

"What am I? The maid?" Her eyes popped out almost as much as Mr. Schneider's. Maybe she was

4

also part spider. "You can make dinner once in a while too, you know."

"But it's not on my list." I pointed to the paper taped to the refrigerator and read out loud: "*Daniel: Load and unload dishwasher, set and clear table, sweep floor after meals, take out trash.* Nothing about making dinner."

Alice pulled a tray of chicken out of the oven. She gave it a long sniff and put it back in, slamming the door shut. Then she filled a pot with water and put it on the stove.

"Maybe it's time for a new list," she said. "Maybe I should remind Mom and Dad that you're eleven and can handle more stuff. Isn't that what you're always telling them? *Come on, I'm not a little kid anymore. I'm double digits.*"

I grunted. I did say that a lot, but that was because I wanted to hang out with my friends more, not 'cause I wanted to cook.

"If you bring up the list," I said, "you're only going to get stuck with more work." I didn't actually know if that was true, but it was worth a try. Worst-case scenario: Mom and Dad would want a family meeting on Sunday. A family meeting meant a reminder from Dad that he worked a thousand shifts a week at the factory, followed by Mom telling us she saved a million lives every day working as a nurse in the emergency room at Croyfield Memorial Hospital.

Not that I didn't appreciate how hard they worked. It was just that my best friend, Frank, and I wanted to go to the movies on Sunday to see *Star Wars*. Yeah, I saw it last year when it came out. I mean, who didn't? But I wasn't going to pass up a chance to go see it again, especially when it was only back for one weekend. I couldn't risk my plans getting bumped for a stupid chore meeting.

"Nice try, but it's not working on me," Alice said. "It won't work on Mom and Dad either. You're not as cute as you used to be."

"What does that have to do with anything? And, yes, I am." I reached up to my hair and attempted to tame my curls.

"Trust me, you're not. Don't worry, though; the awkward stage only lasts six or seven years."

I bent down to check out my reflection in the metal teapot on the stove. A distorted, stretched-out, wild-haired face with an extra-pointy nose blinked back at me. Alice was right. I wasn't cute at all. When had that changed?

"Don't sweat it. You have some of the same genes I do, so you'll probably turn out halfway decent if you survive. Did you at least remember the challah?"

I pulled the plastic bag out of my backpack. Every Friday on my walk home from school, I stopped at Scholly's Bakery for Dad's weekly challah. Mr. Scholly, an Italian man who barely spoke English, always had it ready for me. He made one loaf a week, and it was always for us, the only Jewish family in Croyfield.

I handed the braided bread to my sister.

"Why's it so flat? What'd you do, sit on it or something?"

"I had it in my book bag."

She shoved the sides together, trying to push it back into a loaf shape, and put it on the cutting board in the center of the table. When it came to religion, my family didn't seem all that into it, but Dad had a thing about his challah. He had to have one every Friday night, no matter what.

Alice took a step back and tilted her head, examining it as if it were a work of art instead of a braided lump of bread. "Better."

She walked over to the refrigerator and scribbled *make salad* on my side of the chore list.

"Hey!" I yelled, but she didn't seem to care. "Why can't we just have TV dinners? We can dump them onto plates and pretend we cooked real food. I won't tell."

"Gross," she said. Then she opened the fridge and threw a head of lettuce and a bag of carrots at me with a smirk.

I would have put up more of a fight, but there was no way I was going to miss my chance to see *Star Wars*, so I chopped lettuce and carrots into bite-sized pieces and tossed everything into one of the bright orange bowls that matched our bright orange dishes. In this house full of dishes, they were the only ones we were allowed to touch.

The digital clock over the stove flipped to 5:50. Dad wouldn't be home for ten more minutes. I ran upstairs to my bedroom before Alice decided I had enough time for another chore.

My Super-Secret Spy Notebook was just where I'd left it, in the third drawer of my desk under my pile of Superman comic books. I'd already solved a bunch of mysteries since I started keeping a Super-Secret Spy Notebook, like why Dad lost his keys twice (he had a hole in his coat pocket) and whether Alice was stealing my Halloween candy (yes). Some mysteries were still unsolved, like what type of meat was in Grandma Esther's stew. I opened to my *Unsolved Mysteries* page and wrote: *Is Mr. Schneider a spider?*

Figuring him out would take some work.

CHAPTER 2
PALACE PLANS

By the time Sunday rolled around, I'd forgotten all about Mr. Schneider and his hairy hands. Well, not completely, but seeing Luke Skywalker and C-3PO were way more important. Frank's mom dropped us off in front of the only movie theater in all of Croyfield, the Picture Palace.

It wasn't a real palace. The building had a fake cutout on the front that was supposed to make it look like one. I knew that 'cause Dad's factory made it. Of course, I wasn't the only one with that insider information. Just about everyone in Croyfield knew someone who worked at the factory. It was the biggest place in the whole town, and it made stuff out of fiberglass like tabletops and car parts and cutouts that looked like palaces. I didn't know what fiberglass was, exactly, other than a hard material made out of a bunch of dangerous chemicals. So dangerous they could kill you. At least that's what I'd overheard Mom say.

We stood in line for our movie tickets at the booth just outside of the entrance. Frank stood on his tiptoes and tried to look over the shoulders of the lady in front of us.

"What are you doing?" I asked.

He pointed to the person sitting behind the glass counter handing out the tickets. I tried to stand on my tiptoes so I could see too, but Frank pulled me back down.

"That's my brother's friend Jill. Just let me do the talking. I'll bet I can get us in for free."

Frank's older brother, Raymond, was seventeen and went to the high school with Alice. I liked Raymond. Sometimes he let Frank and me hang out while his band practiced in their basement. I hoped Raymond's friend Jill was as nice as Raymond. A free movie meant I wouldn't have to spend all my allowance money.

We waited while the woman in front of us at the counter bought her tickets. She had three kids with her who were screaming and jumping around. With a string of tickets in one hand and a still-open wallet in her other, the lady glanced at us and sighed before ushering her crew inside.

"Next!" Jill waved for us to step up to the window. She had long blonde hair that feathered back in the exact same way as the girl from the poster that hung next to Raymond's bed. On her red Picture Palace uniform, she wore a name tag that said *Julie*.

"Hi, Jill," Frank said. His voice sounded way deeper than normal. I elbowed him. He cleared his throat and started over in an even deeper voice. "Uh, I mean, hi, Julie."

"What show?" Julie asked without looking up.

"*Star Wars*," he replied.

She picked up a *Sold Out* sign and hung it over the *Star Wars* poster. "Sorry," she said. "I just sold the last ticket."

"To those little kids?" Frank squealed, his voice back to normal. "But they're too young for that movie."

She shrugged. "It's PG, and they're with their mom."

"Still, can't you get us in? It's me, Frank."

She bought her face in close to the glass and scrunched her eyes and nose together.

"Frank Lanzo." He was back to using that weird deep voice. "Ray's brother."

Julie shook her head and rolled her eyes. "How about *Ice Castles*?"

I moaned. *Ice Castles* was a mushy love story about some girl who wanted to be a figure skater. I knew 'cause Alice and her annoying friend Terri talked about it all the time.

Frank leaned in toward Julie. "Ray said you'd be able to get us in no charge."

Julie sat back into her seat and pointed to the price chart taped to the window. "It's two dollars a ticket." Her gum cracked as she spoke. "You want them or what? You're holding up the line."

"Okay, fine," Frank said. "Two tickets to *Ice Castles*."

"What are you doing?" I whispered as Julie handed him our tickets.

"Just trust me, Danny, okay?" he whispered back, opening the door for me. I almost forgot all about it once I smelled the popcorn. The Picture Palace's snack stand had a giant fiberglass red-and-white-striped bucket next to it, filled with giant fiberglass popcorn—also made in Dad's factory. I once asked Dad if he could make one for my bedroom. That's how cool it was.

Before I could take my stupid *Ice Castles* ticket

from Frank, he handed it to the guy sitting in the doorway, who ripped both tickets in two and handed the stubs back to Frank. "*Ice Castles* is to the right in Theater One. Snacks are straight ahead," he mumbled without making eye contact.

"Thanks," Frank mumbled back. "We didn't notice."

I snorted, 'cause even if you had the worst cold ever and couldn't smell the food, who wouldn't notice a giant fiberglass bucket filled with giant fiberglass popcorn? The guy didn't seem to care, though. He was already tearing someone else's tickets.

"Come on," Frank said.

We each bought a popcorn and a soda. Then Frank headed left.

"Where are you going?" I asked. "The guy said *Ice Castles* was to the right in Theater One."

"It is," Frank said. "And *Star Wars* is in Theater Three to the left. They already checked our ticket. We can just walk in."

"But it's sold out," I reminded him.

"Nah," Frank said. "There are always extra seats for VIPs and stuff. Besides did you see the look Julie gave me when I reminded her I was Ray's brother? Trust me, it's totally cool."

Yeah, I saw the look. It was the same headshake-eye roll combo that Alice had given me a million times, and nothing about it said, *It's totally cool.*

We headed into Theater Three anyway. It was packed. Frank and I walked down the left side, across the front, and back up the right. There wasn't a single empty seat.

"Now what?" I asked.

"We could sit up front on the floor."

Frank always liked to sit as close to the screen as possible. Even when the theater was empty, he sat in the front. He said it made him feel like he was a part of the action. I didn't care one way or the other until my neck started to hurt from craning it for so long. Then I cared.

I followed him back down the aisle. We both sat on the carpet in front of the people sitting in the first row.

"This is perfect," Frank whispered. "No one will notice us."

No one except for the man wearing a Picture Palace uniform who walked up and down the aisle holding a flashlight.

"Tickets," he said when he got to Frank and me.

"The guy at the entrance already checked them," Frank replied.

But the man didn't leave. "Tickets," he repeated.

Frank sighed and handed them over.

"Wrong theater. Your show is on the other side in Theater One." He sounded like he'd already said it a bunch of times that day. Probably to kids just like us.

"Come on," Frank pleaded. "Can't you cut us a break? We paid our money. We really want to see this one. We're not bothering anyone here."

"Sorry," he said. Only he didn't sound sorry at all.

For a moment, Frank looked so mad that I thought he was going to throw his popcorn, but Picture Palace popcorn was too good to waste. We both knew that. Instead, we stomped out of the theater.

"I really thought that would work," Frank said. "Maybe we should wait awhile, you know? We can pretend we're going to the bathroom and then try to sneak back in. That guy's not gonna be standing in there for the whole movie, right? Besides, none of the really good stuff happens in the beginning anyway."

"But what if he catches us again?" I asked. "We could get kicked out—banned! Then what would we do? This is the only movie place in Croyfield."

Frank didn't respond. He just kept walking past the snack stand and over to the right side of the building. He stopped at the door to Theater One.

"Now what are we supposed to do?" I asked Frank. "I don't want to see this stupid ice skating movie, but my dad's not picking us up for two hours."

Frank motioned down the corridor to Theater Two. "Want to check that out?"

On weekends, the Picture Palace played little-kid movies in Theater Two. Being seen in one of those was worse than being seen in *Ice Castles*. I sighed. "I'm not sitting through some baby movie."

"Do you see any babies around?" Frank asked. "Let's just find out what it is."

With my popcorn almost a quarter gone, I walked to the end of the hallway. A movie poster with a picture of a boat floating in the ocean hung next to the door. "*The Bermuda Triangle*?" I asked, reading the title. "What's it about?"

Frank studied the poster, glanced around, and then smiled at me. "I don't know, but check that out." He pointed to the ratings box in the bottom corner of the poster. Where there would normally be a G or PG, there was an NR.

"What does that mean?"

"*Not Rated.*" Frank smiled so wide I could see all of the popcorn stuck in his teeth. It was totally gross, even for me. He shoved another handful in his mouth and continued. "Hey, remember *Jaws*? This takes place in the ocean, so I'll bet it's like that. Except the sharks are probably even bigger and meaner. That's gotta be why it's NR."

"I don't know. Theater Two is the family theater. Something just doesn't make sense," I said.

"Stop thinking so much, will you? Just come on. We don't want another one of those Picture Palace guys to see us." Frank opened the door to the mystery theater and slipped inside before I could say another word.

CHAPTER 3
THEATER TWO

The inside of Theater Two was super dark, so I squinted. Sometimes that helped. I was on the lookout for a seat to slide into before another flashlight guy came by and kicked us out.

As it turned out, Theater Two was empty. At the front of the room, the opening credits of the movie rolled across the screen in giant yellow letters while louder-than-normal cheesy music played in the background.

Frank tossed a handful of popcorn into his mouth and started walking toward his usual spot up front. I followed, brushing my hand along the top of the last chair in each row as we made our way down the sloping aisle. We took the two seats in the middle of the front row and stretched out our legs. That was one of the advantages of sitting here. That and the fact that you could practically see up the actors' noses.

The movie started with a group of people on a vacation-type boat. They were all wearing bathing suits and talking and laughing. Then without any warning, the screen changed to show a bunch of war-type airplanes flying in the sky. Then it flashed back to the people on the boat, then back to the airplanes. The whole thing was kind of making me dizzy. I was just about to say so to Frank when the screen flashed again—this time to an air traffic control tower where a group of men in dark green uniforms huddled around a microphone in front of a huge window. There was also one of those blinking, beeping round radar things. As if all of that wasn't confusing enough, the screen flashed one more time and zoomed in on a scary-faced doll floating in the ocean before flashing back to the people on the boat.

"What's going on? What are they saying?" Frank yelled directly into my ear.

The volume on the movie was extra loud, and that made it kind of hard to hear the actors' words, which almost didn't make sense except it was the truth. I thought about finding a Picture Palace worker to let them know, but then they might ask why we were in the wrong movie.

"Something about airplanes disappearing. But I can't figure out what that has to do with the people on the vacation boat."

"And what's with that weird doll floating in the water?" asked Frank. "And why do they keep showing it?"

"No clue," I answered. "It's starting to give me the creeps. I thought you said this would be better than *Jaws*."

"Well, there's gotta be a shark in that water. It's just waiting for its chance to jump out and attack."

"Right," I said, even though now I wasn't so sure.

I sat back in my seat and ate my popcorn. Two men were standing on the vacation boat, talking about the war planes that had disappeared. About how one second they were there and the next second they weren't. Then they started talking about some other boats and planes that were also gone—only those had gone missing a long time ago, and now nobody could explain the mystery. The only thing they knew was that it had happened over this piece of ocean near Bermuda that formed a triangle.

At least I thought that's what they were saying. It was so loud that every time someone spoke, the walls in the theater rattled.

Frank leaned over to me again. "Planes and boats don't just disappear into thin air like that, do they? Somebody had to see something, right?" he asked.

I thought about it for a second. "Actually, I think I've heard of this before."

"This movie?" Frank raised his eyebrows at me.

"No," I told him. "The thing about ships and planes disappearing over the ocean. Yeah, I remember my dad talking about it. I just didn't know what it was called."

"So it's for real?" Frank shouted. His voice was pretty loud, but it didn't matter since the movie was way louder, and we were the only ones in the theater.

"I think so. I mean, it might be."

"Whoa," Frank said. "But it only happens right over that one patch of water—on that Bermuda Triangle? It doesn't happen in other places, does it?"

I kept my eyes on the screen 'cause I didn't know the answer. And I wondered if the boat in the movie was also real or if it was made up for the film, 'cause something awful was clearly about to happen to it. The *something bad is coming* music was playing, and a little girl on the vacation boat was carrying around the same creepy doll that we'd seen before. Maybe it had belonged to someone on one of the other missing boats or planes. Maybe it was haunted or cursed.

A storm suddenly appeared, and a roaring burst of thunder rumbled across the screen and through the theater. The people on the vacation boat screamed. The walls rattled even more. Frank might have screamed too. He definitely jumped and spilled popcorn all over himself.

"This is dumb," he said, brushing popcorn crumbs off of his shirt. "And there aren't any sharks. I'm leaving."

I stood up with what was left of my own popcorn. "Yeah, okay."

Then I followed him out—even though I had a million unanswered questions about what really happened when something entered the Bermuda Triangle.

CHAPTER 4
MRS. ALBERTINI

Frank and I didn't talk about the movie. After we left Theater Two, Frank walked straight up to the snack stand and convinced the guy to refill his popcorn. Just like that. Then on our way outside to play kick the can in the parking lot while we waited for my dad to pick us up, we spotted the new Space Invaders video game in the corner next to the restrooms. It wasn't the greatest location, but we'd never seen that game before. Not in real life, I mean. I'd seen it plenty of times in the ads in my comic books, and it looked like the coolest thing ever. Turned out it was even better than the coolest thing ever. We spent the next hour shooting aliens and using up all of our quarters. By the time my dad arrived, we'd forgotten all about those missing boats and airplanes.

Except they came back in my dreams.

I was hoping to talk to Frank about the movie the next morning. But when I brought it up on our walk to school, he only shrugged. Then he went on and on about how his brother Raymond was saving up for a jukebox from the money he made bagging groceries at the market, and how he wouldn't have to put coins in it or anything to get the records to play. Then he wondered if he could do something to save up for his own Space Invaders video game that he wouldn't have to put money in either. It wasn't a half-bad idea.

As I headed home from school that afternoon, I heard our neighbor Mrs. Albertini call my name.

"Can you give me a hand, Danny?" she yelled out from her second-story window. "The door's unlocked."

I wanted to pretend I didn't see or hear her. It wasn't that I didn't like Mrs. Albertini; I was just in kind of a hurry. If I didn't get home before Alice, I'd have no chance of watching any of my shows.

"Up here, Danny!" she called again. Half of her tiny body dangled out of the window. Even the tiniest breeze might pull her all the way out, and the last thing Croyfield needed was a little old Italian lady splattered on the middle of the sidewalk.

So I stopped walking. "Be right there, Mrs. Albertini."

Her front door was heavy, and it creaked when I pushed it open. It was probably as old as she was. Not that I knew how old she was, but she had a ton of wrinkles. Her house smelled the same as Grandma Esther's: a combination of cleaning products and stale cheese. I tried to breathe only through my mouth to keep the smell out, 'cause I knew from experience that once it entered your nose, it could take hours to leave.

Mrs. Albertini was already in the foyer waiting for me. I couldn't believe she'd gotten downstairs so fast. "In here." She waved me into the kitchen.

She pointed to a tall cabinet next to the stove. "I don't know why my son insists on putting things on the top shelf where I can't reach them."

Mrs. Albertini's son, Anthony, owned the market three blocks away. Mom complained every week about his prices, but she shopped there anyway 'cause she swore he had the best corned beef on the East Coast. I thought it was pretty good, but I didn't think it was the best. Once, when my pop-pop was still alive, he took me into the city for a ball game. Afterward, we stopped for corned beef sandwiches at some tiny deli. That corned beef was *really* good.

"He waits until I'm not paying attention," Mrs. Albertini continued, sliding over a step stool that only gave her a small boost off of the ground. "And then he puts everything where I can't reach it." She shook her head. "Not that I don't appreciate him coming over here once a week with groceries for his mama. He's a good boy, my Anthony. And good boys take care of their mamas." She reached over and took my chin in the palm of her hand. "You're a good boy too, Danny. Make sure you stay that way."

"Yes, Mrs. Albertini." I glanced at the step stool again, then at the top of the cabinet. I was the same height as Mrs. Albertini. If she couldn't reach up there on her stool, I wasn't going to be able to either. "Can I use one of those chairs?" I pointed to the dining set in the corner of the kitchen. The table looked like the ones made in Dad's factory, but the chairs were metal and had shiny plastic-covered seat cushions that made fart sounds every time you sat down and got up. Grandma Esther used to have the same set before she moved into the nursing home. That's how I knew. Maybe that's where the stale cheese smell came from.

"Take your shoes off first," Mrs. Albertini replied.

"And your coat. You'll get overheated and then catch a chill when you go back outside. It's nippy out there today."

It was actually super warm out. Mom said it was 'cause the groundhog saw its shadow, and Dad said it was 'cause of all the pollution from the factory. All I knew was that it was the middle of March, and I'd already traded in my winter coat for my zippered sweatshirt.

Mrs. Albertini watched as I followed her instructions. Then I pulled one of the chairs over, being careful not to scrape it across the floor.

I climbed up and opened the top cabinet. "What am I looking for?" I asked.

"Lokshen."

"What?"

"Lokshen," she repeated. "Egg noodles. The skinny ones. Doesn't your mother cook with them?"

"I don't know. Maybe. She doesn't make a lot of Italian food. Well, except lasagna. Her lasagna is really good." I found the package Mrs. Albertini wanted and handed it to her before getting off of the chair.

"This isn't for an Italian dish. It's for my homemade chicken soup. A secret recipe handed down from my great-great bubbe."

"Bubbe?"

"Yes," Mrs. Albertini said. "Don't you call your grandmother Bubbe?"

"No," I told her. "She's just Grandma. But my dad called his Bubbe. I just didn't know Itali—I mean, I thought only Jewi . . ."

"I am Jewish," Mrs. Albertini interrupted.

"You are?" I asked.

She nodded. "I wasn't always Lola Albertini. A long time ago, I was Lillian Gerstein."

"What happened?" I asked.

She laughed. "I married Mr. Albertini. That's what happened. And he started calling me Lola. Well, it's a long story. Not one that would interest a young boy."

"What about Anthony?" I asked. "Does that mean he's Jewish, too?"

I waited for her to answer my question, but she didn't. She only said, "Thank you for being so helpful, Danny. How about a treat? I've got Scholly's pound cake with chocolate frosting." Mrs. Albertini put a teakettle full of water on the stove and then bent down to pull a large pot from a bottom cabinet. She filled that with water, too.

The clock read 3:15. I still had a fighting chance

of getting to the television before Alice. But Mom hardly ever bought Scholly's pound cake, and the one with chocolate frosting was my favorite. I put the chair back by the table and took a seat. Sure enough, it made the fart sound.

"Mrs. Albertini?" I asked.

She joined me at the table with two thick slices of cake. "Yes, Danny?"

"Have you ever heard about the Bermuda Triangle?"

I don't know why I brought it up, except it was still on my mind, and Frank didn't seem to want to talk about it. I didn't blame him, honestly. The whole thing was pretty weird. Plus, that doll had been *the* creepiest doll I'd ever seen.

Maybe Mrs. Albertini knew something about it. She was old and probably knew about a lot of stuff.

"Oh, sure," she said. "I remember hearing about a whole fleet of planes that vanished over the ocean. A few ships, too. That was back in the forties, I think. Don't tell me it's happened again. One would have to be a brave soul to travel through those waters."

"No," I told her. "It was just something I saw at the movies. So it's real? I thought it might be, but I wasn't sure."

She walked over to the stove and poured her tea. Then she sat back down with me. "That's what they say. It's one of the great mysteries of our time."

"Yeah," I agreed and finished the rest of my cake.

When I got home, Alice was already watching TV.

I raced upstairs to my bedroom, opened the third drawer of my desk, and reached under the fifth comic book in the pile to grab my Super-Secret Spy Notebook. On the *Unsolved Mysteries* page, directly under *Is Mr. Schneider a spider?*, I wrote *Bermuda Triangle*.

CHAPTER 5
WHITE VAN GUY

Nicholas Russo always picked me for his kickball team at recess. He said it was 'cause we'd been friends since before kindergarten. I knew it was really 'cause he had a crush on Alice. I overheard him tell Bobby Caldon one day in the school cafeteria. He told Bobby that he winked at her once and that Alice winked back. Said it was a sure sign she had a crush on him too. I knew for a fact Alice would rather die than be caught hanging out with a sixth-grader. She probably just had something in her eye. Not that I would tell Nicholas that. Getting picked to play kickball at recess was too important.

"Heads up, Wexler!"

My eyes locked on the incoming ball. A catch before a bounce would bring in our third out. We'd been standing in the outfield forever. Now was my chance. I reached out—

My body slammed to the ground.

Nicholas stood over me. Frank chased the rolling ball as Bobby safely made it to second base. "Hey! That was my ball." I wiped the tiny pebbles from the blacktop off of my hands while I sat there.

"You weren't anywhere near it," Nicholas argued. "I was closer."

"Then why'd you have to knock me over to try to get it?" I asked.

"Sorry," he said, reaching to help me up.

The end-of-recess bell rang before we had another chance to get our third out. We all crowded back inside.

"Did you hear about the kid over in Mayson?" Nicholas asked as we headed down the hallway back to our classroom. We were supposed to walk silently in single file, but our teacher, Mrs. Greely, had given up on that rule a while ago.

"What kid?" I said. Mayson was a few towns over, but news from there usually traveled to Croyfield pretty fast.

"The one who disappeared," Nicholas said. "Some eight-year-old boy."

"Disappeared?"

"Well, not into thin air," Nicholas replied. He leaned in closer and explained, "They think he was kidnapped. By the white van guy."

Last year, a nine-year-old girl who lived an hour away claimed she was walking home from school when a guy in a white van pulled up next to her and asked directions. She said that when she walked over to talk to the driver, the sliding door on the side opened, and a giant arm reached out and tried to grab her. But she pulled away and screamed, and the van sped away. Since then, a bunch more kids had said it happened to them too. Some were even close to Croyfield. Same exact thing each time: white van, sliding side door, arm reaching out, and kid running away. This was the first time I'd heard of someone actually getting kidnapped, though.

"So White Van Guy's real," I whispered. Dad had convinced me he wasn't. He said that there were never any witnesses and that kids make stuff up for attention all the time. Mom agreed but then reminded me never to talk to strangers, especially strangers in cars or vans.

"Let's go, boys." Mrs. Greely stood holding our classroom door open.

We hurried in and took our seats.

While we'd been out at recess, Mrs. Greely had written a ton of stuff on the chalkboard. She tapped on it with her ruler. "Eyes up front, everyone."

She might not have cared about the recess line, but she cared plenty about her classroom. We all quieted down. Especially since there was another recess later that she could take away from us.

Mrs. Greely began explaining our next assignment. "For this project, you'll each get to pick one US president for a research report. The list of presidents is here on the board . . ."

"Psst."

Frank's desk was next to mine. He dropped a folded piece of paper to the floor and slid it over to me with his foot.

Mrs. Greely continued to read off the board with her back to the class. "There are enough presidents for each of you to choose someone different . . ."

I reached down to pick up the paper and unfolded it, keeping it on my lap: *Bermuda Triangle.*

I wrote back: *What?* I folded the paper back up before carefully sliding it across the floor over to Frank.

He scribbled some words and then slid it again

toward me. Mrs. Greely turned around. She stared directly at me, so I started copying down the stuff from the board.

"It's due in a month," she said, smiling. "But remember there's a week of spring break stuck in there, and we're not supposed to assign homework over your vacation, so really, you only have three weeks to work on it. Are there any questions?"

Maria Martona, who sat on the other side of the room, raised her hand.

"Yes?" Mrs. Greely asked, even though we all already knew what Maria was about to ask.

"Can we work in pairs?"

That was always her question. Ever since kindergarten. No matter what the assignment. I was so busy thinking about how Maria always wanted to work in pairs that I'd forgotten all about the note on the floor. Frank coughed. Then he motioned for me to pick up the folded piece of paper.

"No, Maria," Mrs. Greely responded. "You'll each pick your own president and do your own report."

I quickly snatched the paper.

"Anyone else?" She waited. Nobody raised a hand. "Well," she said, grabbing the erasers, "I've prepared a handout for you, so don't worry if you haven't copied this down." She turned her back to us again and erased all the notes. "Let's take out our math books now."

While my classmates fumbled around in their desks, I quickly unfolded the note.

White Van Guy isn't real. The Bermuda Triangle is.

I had so many questions. Way more than I could fit on a tiny piece of paper. When the next recess bell rang, I stayed close to Frank and kept my voice low.

"What did your note mean?" I asked. "Are you talking about the kid who disappeared?"

"Yeah," Frank said. "I don't buy it."

"You don't think that kid disappeared?"

"No, that kid is gone all right. I just think there's a lot more to the story."

"So—what—you think the kid somehow got sucked up in the Bermuda Triangle?"

Frank shrugged. "I've been doing research."

"What kind of research?" I asked.

"What are you talking about?" Nicholas elbowed me into Frank as he asked me the question.

He always did that, and he wasn't trying to be mean or anything, it was just kind of his thing. Usually it bugged me. But this time, I didn't mind it so much 'cause it gave Frank a chance to whisper, "I'll tell you later," into my ear.

"We're just talking about this president project," Frank told Nicholas.

"Speaking of that," Nicholas said, "what are you doing after school, Danny? My mom's nosey friends are coming over for their weekly card game. You know how they get—always asking a bunch of annoying questions. Do you think I can come over? To work on my president project? A month isn't very long."

Nicholas and I hung out after school all the time, so I knew this had nothing to do with getting a head start on schoolwork and everything to do with seeing Alice. But Frank didn't seem like he wanted to share this Bermuda Triangle stuff, and I really wanted to hear what he had to say, so I thought of the one thing that might make Nicholas change his mind.

"Sure," I told Nicholas. "It'll be super quiet at my house. Alice has dance lessons today. We can get a lot done on our project."

He concentrated on the pebble he'd been kicking between his feet. "Actually, now that I think about it, I forgot that my mom canceled the game to take me to an appointment. I'll come tomorrow instead."

"Yeah, okay," I told him. "Tomorrow."

"Are we playing kickball or what?" Nicholas asked. "Come on, before Joey decides he wants to be captain."

I didn't even want to play kickball. I wanted to talk to Frank. But I couldn't risk losing my spot on the team. I gave Frank a tiny nod to let him know we'd finish later and took my usual position in the outfield.

CHAPTER 6
SERIOUS THEORIES

The house was empty when I arrived home from school. Mom had left a note on the kitchen table to say she'd taken Alice to dance class. She always left a note even though I *knew* Alice had dance every Tuesday. I grabbed a handful of chips from the pantry and waited for the knock on the door. Frank showed up about twenty minutes later.

"Check this out," he said. The bright red encyclopedia landed on the kitchen table with a thud. Frank's mom had bought a complete set of encyclopedias for their family back when Raymond started junior high school. She said they'd need it for their assignments, and you couldn't count on the set at the library 'cause people didn't always put the books back in the right place or they kept the one you needed way too long. It happened to me all the time, and I wasn't even in junior high school yet.

When I asked my mom for a set, she said that it cost as much as a month's worth of food and that if she had that much extra money, there was a long list of stuff she'd spend it on before she bought a set of books we could easily get at the library. Or, I guess, from Frank.

He opened to a page that had a picture of the ocean with a triangle drawn above it and a heading in big black letters:

THE BERMUDA TRIANGLE

"Told you it was real," Frank said. "Encyclopedias don't lie."

The information below it took up two whole pages. I couldn't take my eyes off the picture of the airplanes in the middle of the second page. They were exactly like the ones that had disappeared in the movie.

The paragraph under the picture talked about the planes and boats that went missing and said the whole thing was still a big mystery.

Frank shoved his hands in his pants pocket and

pulled out a wad of crumpled-up paper. "There's more." He flattened out the creases. "Yesterday at the library, the front desk lady helped me find this article in a magazine. A real-life scientist wrote it. I read it and took a bunch of notes while my mom was deciding which book she wanted to check out."

The title was "The Real Truth about the Bermuda Triangle."

"So what did you find out?" I asked.

"This scientist guy did a bunch of studies," Frank started. He was talking in a real low voice even though no one was home. "And he came up with two possible explanations. The first one is that the lost city of Atlantis is buried deep in the ocean in the exact spot of the Bermuda Triangle."

"What's the lost city of Atlantis?"

"It's a place that sank into the ocean like a million years ago. No one really knows what happened. Maybe it was 'cause of an earthquake."

"Or a meteor," I suggested. "Like what some people say happened with the dinosaurs."

"Maybe. Anyway, the details are a little sketchy. Like no one knows where in the ocean it is. There aren't exactly any maps and encyclopedias from a million years ago."

"What does all that have to do with the Bermuda Triangle?" I asked.

"People say Atlantis has magical powers and can shoot energy beams from old fire crystals."

"How's it do that?"

"That part is also a little sketchy," Frank said. "But the guy who wrote the article thinks it could explain all the missing planes and boats."

"And that would explain the disappearing kid from Mayson?" I asked.

"No," Frank began. "But his other explanation could."

Alice opened the front door and slammed it shut before I could ask another question. She stormed into the kitchen.

"What are you doing home?" I demanded. So what if I sounded a little rude? She was barging in on Frank and me in the middle of an important, private conversation. Maybe she would go sulk in her room and leave us alone. Instead, she plopped herself in a chair. Right there at the table with Frank and me.

"Mom dropped me off. I didn't want to stay at dance."

I knew asking why would be a bad move. A really, really bad move. So I slowly pushed back my chair and tried to make eye contact with Frank to get him to follow my lead. If we played this right, we could escape to my bedroom. My chair scraped against the linoleum floor as I stood.

"Why didn't you want to stay?" Frank asked her.

Shoot. I sat back down.

"Madame Robin gave out the parts for our spring performance today. Do you know what part I got?" Alice crossed her arms. She glared at me as if whatever had happened in dance today was all my fault.

"N-n-no."

"I'm *girl walking across stage.* Ten years of dance class and I'm *walking.* It's a five-second part. Meanwhile, Gloria Amato, who has only taken dance for two years, gets the lead. She's onstage for practically the entire two-hour performance. And you know why, don't you?"

"She's better?" I responded.

Alice's glare morphed into something horrible. I pushed my lips together super tightly, determined not to say another word that would make her face any worse.

"No, birdbrain," she said. "It's because her last name is Amato and my last name is Wexler."

I glanced at Frank as I thought about this. He was curling up the corners of the crumbled piece of paper with his fingers.

"You're not going to say anything?"

That had been my plan. But since she was insisting on something, I said, "Your teacher assigned the parts alphabetically?" This time, I really wasn't trying to be rude. I was only trying to figure out why our last name made a difference.

"No!" Alice rolled her eyes. "I'm Jewish, and she's not."

"What does that have to do with anything?" I asked.

She sighed. "Think about it. Why do you think Dad's never gotten a promotion after all these years at the factory? Mr. Martona was promoted. So was your friend Nicholas's dad. Gloria Amato's mom. Heck, even Frank's dad has had two promotions now. He's one of Dad's bosses."

Frank refused to meet my eyes.

Alice continued. "But not our dad. He's had the same job since he and Mom moved here almost twenty years ago. Since before both of us were born."

"Maybe he likes that job," I suggested.

Alice shook her head. "It's not just that. Haven't you noticed how Mom and Dad never talk about being Jewish with anyone other than Grandma Esther?"

"They like to keep it low key," I said. "Because we're not religious."

"Is that why Dad keeps a prayer book in his nightstand?"

"You shouldn't be snooping through his drawers," I said.

"I wasn't. He showed it to me. When I turned thirteen. The same way he'll show it to you. In private, without anyone else knowing."

"I don't get it."

"Look around you, Danny. People may smile at us, but that doesn't mean they like us living here. I'm not making this up. It's real." She stopped. "No offense, Frank. I know *you* like us."

Frank shifted in his chair. "I think I hear my mom calling me."

"But you live three blocks away," I said.

"Yeah, that's definitely her. I really have to go." He stood up, grabbed his encyclopedia and crumpled paper, and headed toward the front door.

"Don't listen to Alice," I whispered, following him. "She didn't mean all that stuff. You know how she is; when she gets mad about something, she doesn't know when to shut up."

"It's fine. Don't sweat it." He opened the door. "I'll see you tomorrow."

"Wait," I said. "What about the scientist guy and the Bermuda Triangle? You never told me the second explanation."

A sly smile crossed Frank's lips. "Aliens."

CHAPTER 7
ALIEN MONKEY BUSINESS

Between Alice's rant and Frank's Bermuda Triangle theory, my mind was racing. Three times during the night, I pulled out my Super-Secret Spy Notebook to check out my latest entry: *Aliens*. Was it possible?

To make matters worse, Frank hardly spoke to me the next morning. He didn't even want to play kickball at recess, and Frank *always* wanted to play kickball. He said he had a headache and didn't feel well, but I knew it was 'cause of all that awful stuff Alice had said. Not even a quarter of the way through the game, just as Bobby Caldon stepped up to home plate, I called a time-out.

"What'd you do that for?" Nicholas asked. "Everyone knows Bobby is an easy out."

"I have a headache too," I told him. "I don't want to play anymore."

"But we're in the middle of a game. You just can't leave in the middle of a game. We'll be short a guy."

I shrugged and walked away. There were plenty of kids in sixth grade who wanted to play kickball but never got picked. I didn't care about losing my spot this time.

I headed off to find Frank. I knew he'd be sitting at the top of the old rusty monkey bars along the far side of the school building, where we weren't supposed to be anymore. Two years ago, the school had built a new playground in the back lot. Except they never took the old one down. They just left it to get older and rustier. So Frank and I came here sometimes when we wanted to hang out and be alone. It was our secret spot. Even Nicholas didn't know about it.

Frank's feet dangled between the metal rungs. I climbed up and sat next to him. Neither of us said a word. My feet swayed in the exact same rhythm as his.

"What's the matter?" I asked.

"It's not my dad's fault, you know." He kept his eyes down. Maybe he was noticing how our legs were moving at the exact same pace too.

"What's not?" Gray clouds moved in, covering the last bits of sunshine. They were exactly the sort of clouds I imagined aliens might use to hide behind.

"The stuff about your dad," he continued. "About how he's never gotten a promotion."

"Why would it be your dad's fault?"

Frank stopped swinging his legs and turned to face me. "Because my dad's . . . you know."

"One of the bosses?"

He focused on his feet again. "I guess."

"Nobody thinks it's his fault," I told him.

"Your sister does. And your dad probably does too. Alice even said he only got to be a boss 'cause of his last name. 'Cause he's Italian."

"Who cares what Alice said? She was just mad about all that stupid dance stuff. If you ask me, I'll bet she got that walking part 'cause she opened her big mouth and said something nasty to her dance teacher. She's always being nasty to people. Heck, I'd give her a bad part too, and I'm her brother. Her *Jewish* brother."

He paused for a little bit and then said, "Yeah, okay. I guess you're right."

"I know I am. I already told you it was all dumb."

Frank nodded. Then he went back to swinging his feet right next to mine. Two birds flew above us, chasing each other in circles. Maybe they were best friends.

"Anyway, forget about nosey Alice. I want to hear more about the aliens and the guy who wrote that Bermuda Triangle article."

Frank's lips curled up into a smile, and I knew the headache that wasn't really a headache was over. "Well, he thinks there are these other life-forms out there," he explained. "In the universe."

"Like Martians?" I asked.

"Yeah, exactly. And he thinks they were trying to learn about life here on Earth. So he's saying they may have come here . . ."

"Like in their spaceships?" I interrupted again.

"Right," Frank replied. "In actual UFOs—you know, unidentified flying objects. And they would fly over that patch of ocean over Bermuda and— ZAP!" He threw his arms straight up into the air and wiggled his fingers. "The Martians would zap the planes and boats right onto the spaceships. That's how come they vanished without a trace."

"How did all those boats and planes fit? On their spaceships, I mean?"

"I don't know," Frank said. "Maybe they had some kind of shrinking device or something."

I nodded. In a weird way, it all kind of made sense. "So what did they do next?" I asked. "After they zapped up the boats and planes?"

Frank shrugged again. "I guess they took them back to whatever planet they're from. The scientist guy who wrote the article didn't really go into details."

I looked back up to the clouds. "Do you believe him? This scientist guy?"

"He sounded pretty smart," Frank replied, "and the article said he'd been studying this stuff for a long time." He picked at a piece of peeling, rusted paint on the monkey bars. "Of course, it's only a theory. Same as the lost city of Atlantis. He hasn't been able to prove anything."

"But he must have something. A person can't just spout any old thing that comes to their head and expect people to believe it." I wanted to use all that nonsense my sister said yesterday as an example, but I wasn't about to bring it up again. Not when Frank was finally back to his normal self.

"Exactly," Frank said. "That's why I think he's actually on to something—and why it might be connected to that kid in Mayson."

"But Nicholas said the kid from Mayson was kidnapped by White Van Guy," I reminded him.

"Nobody's ever seen White Van Guy," Frank pointed out. "Just like nobody's seen the aliens."

"And that's why you think White Van Guy isn't real?"

"I guess *real* isn't the right word," Frank corrected. "He's not human, is what I meant."

"Are you saying White Van Guy's one of the aliens?" I took a couple of seconds to think this over. "But we're nowhere near the Bermuda Triangle."

"Maybe they've moved to a different part of the world. Maybe they have enough boats and planes, and now they want little kids." Frank looked at me with a super-serious stare.

"Whoa." I suddenly felt both excited and scared all at the same time. The hairs on my arms got tingly, and I kind of wished we weren't sitting all by ourselves. I also wished I had my Super-Secret Spy Notebook with me so I could write all this down. "A real-life Martian driving around, snatching kids off of the street."

"Exactly. And that's probably why nobody's seen this white van. As soon as they grab a kid, the UFO zaps them up."

I swung my legs faster while I thought that over. "So how come all those other kids got away?" I asked. "Don't Martians have superpowers? They had no problem with ships and boats."

"The Martians were probably still working on their technology. Even they're not perfect. Plus, little kids are, you know, little. They make harder targets. It'd be kind of embarrassing to miss a whole fleet of airplanes."

He had a good point. "So where do you think he is now?" I asked, back to studying the clouds. "The kid from Mayson? Do you think he's on some faraway planet hanging out with other kids who've been zapped up?"

"Don't forget all the people on those boats and ships, too."

"Right. But why would the Martians want so many people?"

The bell for the end of recess sounded before Frank could answer, and I was kind of glad it did. I had enough things keeping me up at night.

CHAPTER 8
THE ALMOST PROMOTION

After school, I stopped at Mrs. Albertini's house and rang the bell. I'd never done that before. At least, I'd never done it without Mom asking me to drop something off or help with some other chore. This time, I didn't really have a reason. I just did it.

When Mrs. Albertini opened the door, I braced myself for the killer cleaning products and stale cheese combo stench, but instead, her house smelled like hamburgers and onions. My stomach growled.

"Come in, Danny, come in." Her flowery dress had short sleeves, large pockets in the front, and a long zipper that went straight down the middle. It was the same kind of dress that all the old ladies in the neighborhood wore. Hers was so big that she could probably fit three other people in there with her.

I thought she would seem surprised or ask me what I was doing there, but instead, she acted as if she'd been expecting me. She even had two slices of Scholly's chocolate-frosted pound cake already waiting at the kitchen table.

"Do you always put out two plates of cake?" I asked. If Mom were here, she probably would have given me an elbow or her sideways eye to let me know it was a rude question. Maybe it wasn't the politest thing to say, but I was curious, and it was too late to take it back.

"No," Mrs. Albertini answered without any further explanation. Then she poured lemonade for me. I sat down in the farting chair by the window and took a sip.

"Thanks," I said, in case she was annoyed about that last question, but also 'cause I knew I should say it anyway.

"How are you, Danny?" she asked.

"Okay, I guess."

"That was always the answer my Anthony would give when something was troubling him. Is there anything on your mind?"

I shoved a forkful of cake in my mouth and gulped it down. The wrinkles around Mrs. Albertini's eyes were all perfectly spaced, kind of like the rings in a tree's trunk. We'd learned in science class that you could tell how old a tree was based on those rings. I knew that wasn't true for humans, but I had a feeling Mrs. Albertini's wrinkles were plenty old. She did remember all those planes and boats disappearing in the Bermuda Triangle, and that happened a really long time ago.

"Did Mr. Albertini work at the factory?" I took another huge bite of cake followed by a swig of lemonade.

"Absolutely," Mrs. Albertini answered. "He worked there from the day he got out of the army. Just about everyone here did. Still do as a matter of fact. It's the heart of Croyfield. That and my Anthony's market, of course."

"And Scholly's Bakery," I said, my mouth still full.

"Yes," she laughed. "We can't forget about Scholly's Bakery."

"But when Mr. Albertini worked at the factory," I said, making sure not to put more food in my mouth while talking, "did he—I mean, did his boss . . ."

"What is it, Danny? You don't have to be shy with me."

"Well, it's just . . . when he worked there, did he ever get promoted?"

A huge smile formed across Mrs. Albertini's lips, pushing the wrinkles around her mouth up toward her ears. "He most certainly did. Worked himself all the way up to head production manager. Not bad for a kid who never finished high school." Her eyes shifted to a shelf above the sink, where a framed black-and-white photo of a man in an army uniform sat between two fancy plates on stands. Apparently, Mrs. Albertini collected fancy plates too. "We were all so proud of him." Then she looked me straight in the eyes. "But you need to stay in school. Yes?"

"Yes, ma'am," I replied. As long as she was giving me chocolate-frosted cake, I'd pretty much do whatever she told me to do. "Can I ask you something else?"

"Of course." She stood up and walked over to the kitchen counter. "Come. You can help me roll cabbage. It's Anthony's favorite, and I promised I'd make some for him."

"I don't know how to cook." I finished the rest of my cake in one bite before walking over to stand next to her.

"I'll show you. It's easy." She pulled over a pan

lined with big cabbage leaves, took a spoonful of the chopped-up meat, rice, and onions I'd smelled, and dropped it into the center of one of the leaves. "My mother taught me how to make this when I was your age. It's easiest if you fold in the short ends first, then roll the long ends." She demonstrated on the one she'd started, then handed me the spoon. "Go ahead and try."

I did what she said, but my cabbage tore as soon as I started to roll it. Meat spilled over the edges.

"I'm no good at this," I groaned.

Mrs. Albertini laughed. "I've torn many pieces of cabbage in my day. The trick is not to overstuff. It takes practice to get just the right amount in there, but don't fret. It will still taste delicious."

I watched carefully as she rolled the next few pieces. Then she had me try again on the last leaf. I used less filling this time. It still didn't look right.

"You said you wanted to ask me something else?" Mrs. Albertini said. She filled her teakettle with water and put it on the stove to heat up.

I handed the spoon back to her. "It's about the factory. Did the other people who worked there get promoted too?"

"Well, I don't know about everyone." She took

a can of crushed tomatoes out of the cabinet. "But many did. Mind you, they didn't all rise to senior management. It took Mr. Albertini many years and a lot of hard work to get to that spot. It wasn't easy, and the factory did have its share of rough patches. There were plenty of years where there weren't any promotions at all and years where people lost jobs too. But for the most part, the factory has been very good to the people of Croyfield. Even in difficult times."

I nodded, watching as she opened the can and poured the tomatoes on top of the cabbage rolls.

"Is that what's worrying you?" she asked. "Is there talk of money troubles at the factory? I still have a few friends down there, although not as many now that Mr. Albertini is gone. But I haven't heard any rumors of layoffs. Is your father worried about losing his job?"

"No," I said. "It's nothing like that. I mean, he hasn't mentioned anything."

"Good." She smiled again, and this time, the wrinkles around her eyes scrunched together like a pack of squiggly worms. She added a bunch of other ingredients to the pan and put it in the oven. "But something's still troubling you."

I looked away from Mrs. Albertini and her

wrinkles. "My dad's been working at the factory for twenty years. He's never gotten a promotion. My sister says it's 'cause he's Jewish."

The kettle on the stove started to smoke and whistle. Mrs. Albertini walked over to it and poured her tea. Then she sat back down at the table and sighed. I joined her.

"Mr. Albertini had hoped to change all that once he made it to senior management," she said.

"So what my sister said is true?" Nothing could fill the sudden pit in my stomach. Not even another slice of pound cake. "But that's not fair."

"You're right. And Mr. Albertini understood that better than anyone. He even put in a promotion recommendation for your father. He knew it would be difficult, and he was prepared to fight. He wanted so much to improve things."

"But my dad didn't get promoted. He's *never* gotten promoted. Why couldn't Mr. Albertini make it happen?"

Mrs. Albertini stood up again. This time, it was to walk over to the sink, where she picked up the photo on the shelf.

"He died," she said sadly. "My Gino died."

CHAPTER 9
MISTAKES AND MIX-UPS

On the way home from Mrs. Albertini's house, I remembered it was Wednesday, so Mom was working late at the hospital. I also remembered I now had to help Alice with the dumb salad for dinner. I ran the rest of the way home and nearly knocked Mom over as I rushed through the front door.

"What's the hurry?" she asked. "Dinner's not ready yet."

"What are you doing here?" I followed her into the kitchen. The calendar hung on the wall next to the phone. Wednesday. Yeah, just as I'd thought.

"I switched shifts. Dinner in ten minutes. Don't go too far."

With just enough time to update my Super-Secret Spy Notebook, I ran upstairs and carefully pulled it out from under my Superman comic. I stared at the *Unsolved Mysteries* page. Frank was definitely on to something, so I drew a double-headed arrow to link *Aliens* to *Bermuda Triangle*. Then I drew another double-headed arrow and linked all of that to my next entry:

White van kidnapper/Missing Mayson kid

Then, on a separate line without any arrows, I added another entry:

Dad's promotion

A few minutes later, I heard Dad come home from work.

At dinner, I barely had any appetite, and it had nothing to do with the food I'd eaten at Mrs. Albertini's house earlier. I just couldn't get her words out of my head. It didn't help that Dad was all steamed up about some problem at the factory. I pushed around half-eaten pieces of meatloaf and dug swirly tunnels through my pile of mashed potatoes. The watery gravy slid through like a waterslide on a muddy day.

"So then the two bosses on the shift, Lanzo and Santone, came down and examined everything," Dad said as he cut his meatloaf into perfect bite-sized pieces. "Of course, none of it was any good, so we had to start the process all over again."

Dad always liked to cut his food before he started eating. Everyone else I knew cut as they went, but not Dad. He had to have it all ready to go before his first bite, even if it was soft like meatloaf.

"Can you imagine?" he continued, his eyes on his food. "Every machine powered down, all materials scrapped. Half the project was done too. All because some idiot in preproduction read the order wrong."

"Howard, language," Mom warned. "And Danny, stop playing with your food and eat it. Did you practice your piano today?"

"Not yet, Mom."

"Mr. Schneider's coming on Friday for your lesson."

"I know. I'll practice." I put three green beans on my fork and waited.

"Sorry, Howie," Mom said. "What happened next?"

As soon as Mom turned away, I dumped the green beans back on my plate.

"Well," Dad continued, "we had to start over. We couldn't send the client a stack of tabletops that were only a foot wide. Who can sit at a twelve-inch table?" Dad pretended he was scrunching his body up to shrink it into a tiny ball. "Any idi—" He glanced at Mom. "Any *person* could see that was a mistake. So I took it upon myself to pull the original order sheet. They should have been twenty-four inches, not twelve. Not only that, they were supposed to be gray and white, not green and white. For the Harvest Bistro no less. That's one of our biggest customers."

"Way to go, Dad. You saved the day," Alice said. She grabbed her plate and walked it over to the sink.

Mom cleared her throat.

"Can I be excused?" Alice asked in her *I'm secretly rolling my eyes* voice.

"Your father's in the middle of a story," Mom said.

"I have homework."

"It's fine." Dad waved her away. "Anyway, management should have been thanking me for finding such a big mistake, but instead, Santone yelled at me."

"Why would he yell at *you*?" Mom asked. "This wasn't your fault."

"He sure acted like it was. Kept spouting off about all the time and money wasted because we had to start over." He stabbed four cuts of meatloaf on his fork and ate them all at once. "The only one who stuck up for me was Lanzo. He's a good guy. So's his kid, Frank." Dad smiled at me.

"The whole family is lovely," Mom added. "We should have them over." She put another spoonful of green beans on my plate. I swirled them into my mashed potato mudslide. Maybe Mom wouldn't notice.

"Next time, I'll just keep my mouth shut," Dad continued. "Let someone else take the heat."

"No, you won't," Mom said. "You always do the right thing. And we're proud of you for it."

"That's not going to get me a promotion," he said.

"You almost had one," I blurted.

"What?" he asked.

"A long time ago. Before Mr. Albertini died." As soon as the words popped out of my mouth, I wondered if telling Dad what I knew was a mistake. Maybe finding out how close he'd come to a promotion would only make him feel worse.

"What are you talking about, Danny?" Mom asked.

"I . . ." I glanced around the table. Both Mom's and Dad's eyes were on me. Maybe those Bermuda Triangle white van aliens would zap me up, right here out of my kitchen, 'cause now would be a really good time for that to happen.

"Did you know Mrs. Albertini is Jewish?" I asked. Maybe if I started there, I could distract them.

"Yes," Mom said. She paused, then added, "She converted, didn't she? When she got married?"

"I don't think so," I told her.

"Huh," Mom replied. "I always thought . . ."

"I'm confused," Dad said. "What did you start to say about a promotion?"

"Oh. Just that . . . Mrs. Albertini said her husband thought you should get one. But he died before he had a chance to tell anyone else at the factory."

I don't know why I lied. Maybe I didn't want Dad to feel the same pit in his stomach that I still felt. He'd already had a rotten enough day.

CHAPTER 10
THE PIANO LESSON

After I told Dad about his almost promotion, he and Mom asked me to leave the room. They did that when they had important adult business to discuss. So I went and practiced the piano for exactly one hour just as I'd promised. Alice came out of her room after the first three minutes to complain. The next night, I practiced for another hour. This time, Alice waited fifteen minutes before stomping out of her room. Maybe that meant I was getting better. Both times she slammed her door when Mom told her to get back to her homework.

Friday morning, the phone rang in the middle of breakfast. Dad's face turned white. I thought maybe he was having a heart attack right there at the table over lumpy oatmeal, but then he mumbled,

"Nobody ever calls with good news this early," and he kept on eating while Mom picked up the receiver. Turned out he was right. Nicholas's mom had called to ask if Nicholas could come over to our place after school. His aunt was in the hospital with something that didn't sound so good, and his parents needed to go visit her.

When Frank heard that Nicholas was coming over, he asked me if he could come too. I figured it would be okay, especially after the way Mom and Dad gushed over Frank and his family the other night.

Right after we got to my house, Mr. Schneider the Spider showed up.

His buggy eyes twitched while he stared at Nicholas and Frank down his long, pointy nose. "We have a lesson today, Daniel, don't we?" Tufts of black hair stuck out from beneath the gloves he wore, which was strange since it was another warm day. But if I had spider hands, I guess I'd wear gloves too.

"Uh-huh," I replied.

Nicholas and Frank looked totally freaked out as Mr. Schneider pulled his gloves off. I didn't blame them. I was kind of freaked out myself. I fake-coughed to get their attention.

"Oh, right," Frank said to Nicholas. "Come on." They headed to the couch across the room and started playing cards.

Mr. Schneider sat next to me at the piano. After I played what I'd practiced, my spider teacher didn't say a word. Nothing. He only pulled out the music for the next part of the song from his briefcase.

I stared at his fingers on the keys and tried extra hard to concentrate on what he was playing, but my mind wandered back to the whole spider business, and I started to wonder if Frank would lend me his *T* encyclopedia so I could look up *tarantulas*. That's when I glanced across the living room to where Frank and Nicholas were *supposed* to be playing cards.

Instead, they were staring right at us. They kept their hands tight over their mouths as they tried to hold in their laughter. I furrowed my brow at them. A loud snicker escaped Frank's mouth. That made Nicholas burst out laughing. I never should have told them I thought Mr. Schneider was part spider.

"Something funny, boys?" Mr. Schneider turned to face my friends. His eyes bulged so far out of his head that I thought they might pop out and roll across the floor.

Nicholas and Frank both cleared their throats

and pretended to be concentrating on the cards in their laps. Except they couldn't stop giggling. "No, sir. It sounds great."

Mr. Schneider shifted back to me. "Perhaps your friends would be more comfortable in the kitchen?"

"Right," I said, giving them the signal to get out.

They took their cards and left the room. Mr. Schneider started the song over. He almost made it through the entire thing, but just before the end, Frank and Nicholas returned—this time followed by Alice.

She walked straight over to me and put her face directly into mine. "I'm trying to make dinner, and your creepy friend here keeps getting in my way."

Mr. Schneider grabbed his notebook off of the top of the piano and slid it into his briefcase. Then he stood up.

"You're leaving?" I asked. "But my lesson just started."

"No, it's over," Mr. Spider Schneider replied. He picked up the jacket that he'd placed on the back of the chair next to the television and slipped the gloves over his hairy hands. "Tell your mother to call me during the week." Then he picked up the envelope Mom had left with his payment for a full lesson. He shoved it into his coat pocket before marching out of the front door.

"What's his problem?" Frank asked.

I shrugged.

"Way to scare off another piano teacher," Alice said. "At least you didn't kill this one with your dragon breath."

"I didn't kill Mr. Tomlin," I told her. "He had cancer!"

She ignored this, planting her hands on her hips. "Listen, I've got to finish dinner before Dad gets home. It's bad enough that I have to do everything around here when Mom works late, but now I've got to cook for two extra people." Her death stare shifted over to my friends.

"I can help," Nicholas offered.

"You can help by staying out of the kitchen," Alice replied. She turned back to me. "Just give me the challah."

I froze.

On the way home from school, I'd been so focused on talking to Nicholas and Frank that I'd walked right past Scholly's Bakery without thinking about how it was Friday.

"Daniel, did you hear me? Give me Dad's challah."

"I—I don't have it. I forgot."

"How could you forget?" Alice yelled. "It's the only job you have."

She rolled her eyes and grabbed her jacket from the closet next to the door. "Never mind. Apparently, if you want something done around here, you have to do it yourself. Just start the salad, and do not touch anything else in the kitchen. Got it?"

I was about to remind her that making the salad was also one of my jobs, but before I could say anything, Nicholas jumped off of the couch, grabbed his sweatshirt, and yelled, "I'll go with you!"

Alice turned to sneer at him. "Ew, no." Then she left and slammed the door shut behind her.

Nicholas stood there still facing the door with a weird goofy smile frozen on his face, while I turned on the television and sat on the couch with Frank. A salad took five minutes to make. I could do it in a little bit.

"*. . . and still no word on eight-year-old Patrick Jamison or the white van involved in his disappearance,*" the man on the TV said. "*Police are asking for any and all leads to be called in to the number at the bottom of the screen. A reward of two thousand dollars will be given for useful information.*"

"Figures," Frank said. "Aliens don't leave behind clues."

Nicholas snapped out of his trance and walked over to us. "What did you say?" he asked.

"Aliens," I repeated, since Frank didn't seem to care about keeping it a secret.

Frank explained everything we knew about the Bermuda Triangle, White Van Guy, aliens, and the missing kid.

After a moment of silence, Nicholas said solemnly, "You know what we need to do, don't you?"

I shook my head.

"Get that two-thousand-dollar reward."

"How?" I asked.

"Find the aliens," Nicholas replied.

CHAPTER 11
SECRETS AND CLUES

I expected Nicholas to crack up after saying we needed to catch the aliens, but his expression stayed dead serious. Not like when he was watching Mr. Spider Schneider and burst out laughing even though he'd tried super hard not to. That's how I knew he wasn't joking about this.

"So you believe it could be aliens?" Frank asked.

Nicholas nodded. "My dad says that when he was a kid, one of those unidentified flying object things crashed out west, and the government captured a bunch of outer space guys from the spaceship. Real-life Martians, you know? He says they're still hidden away, deep in some cave where no one can find them."

I scoffed. "That's a story someone made up to try to get famous. It was just a hot air balloon that crashed. The people who run the space program even said so, and they're the ones who are always out there searching, so they would know."

"They're not going to *tell* us they have aliens," Frank said. "It would cause a national panic. Anyway, I thought you believed in this too."

"I do," I said. "But what do a bunch of Martians captured and hidden away out west have to do with our white van aliens?"

"I don't know," Nicholas said. "Maybe they want to trade. Our people for their people. Or maybe they're totally different and don't have anything to do with these aliens. I'm just saying what my dad said, that's all."

My eyes wandered to the ceiling. Just where were the white van aliens? Were they still hovering above us somewhere? Or were they back at their planet making plans for their next move?

"How would we do it?" I asked. "How would we find the aliens?"

"Not sure," Nicholas admitted.

"Hey, I got a telescope for my birthday last year," Frank offered. "A Spacetron Z7000."

"Whoa," Nicholas said.

"What's so great about a Spacetron Z7000?" I asked.

"Let's just say," Nicholas said, "that if there *is* a UFO out there zapping up a white van with kids in it, like Frank says there is, we'll be able to see it in action."

"That's right," Frank agreed. "And maybe even track them back to whatever planet they're living on. By looking through the telescope, I mean."

"Then what would we do?" I had nothing against this plan so far, but it wasn't like we could jump on our bikes and follow the aliens back to Mars or anything.

"Call the number on the television," Frank said. "Tell the police what we know, and collect our two-thousand-dollar reward."

Before any of us could respond, Alice swung the door open, carrying Dad's challah. "Frank," she said, "I just saw your mom at the bakery. She didn't even know you were at our house. She said to get your butt home and do your chores." She smirked and added, "That makes one less for dinner. Salad done, Danny?" She walked back into the kitchen without waiting for a response.

Frank groaned and stood up. "Guess I forgot to call home to ask if I could stay. Don't start alien hunting without me, though, got it?"

"Yeah, okay." I followed him to the door. "Anyway, you're the one with the telescope, remember?"

"Good point. Call me if anything new happens." I watched through the screen door as Frank disappeared down the street and around the corner.

"Alien hunting?"

I whipped around to see Alice standing in the kitchen doorway.

"What are you doing? Spying on us?" I asked.

"I just came to tell you that you have two minutes to get the salad done, or I'm telling Mom we need a chore meeting this weekend. And you need to set the table too. Dad will be home soon."

I was about to tell Nicholas he could wait in the living room and watch television while I did everything, but he had already jumped up to follow Alice back into the kitchen.

"So why are you two nerds searching for aliens?" Alice grabbed the pitcher of Hawaiian Punch from the refrigerator and put it on the counter. "Trying to conquer Darth Vader so you can save the galaxy?"

"You wouldn't understand," I told her, tearing lettuce into tiny pieces.

"Actually," Nicholas said, "we think the white van that kidnapped the boy in Mayson might be a cover for an alien operation."

"Uh-huh." Alice put the challah on a plate and placed it in the center of the table. "Oh, speaking of white vans, I saw your piano teacher at Scholly's just now."

"Mr. Schneider? What does he have to do with white vans?" I asked.

"He was driving one," Alice said. She went to the oven and pulled out the roast. "Must be hard to drive one of those these days—everyone staring at you, wondering if you're a kidnapper and all. Anyway, he asked Mr. Scholly for some sort of Irish tart. Of course, Mr. Scholly didn't have any. Everyone knows he only bakes Italian stuff. Well, except for Dad's challah." Alice covered the meat in the pan with foil. "Touch my roast before Dad gets home and neither one of you will live to see twelve. And put the salad on the table when you're done. I'll be upstairs." She left the room. I waited until I heard her bedroom door shut.

"Patrick," I said.

"What?" Nicholas asked.

"The boy who was kidnapped. His name was Patrick."

"So?"

"So, didn't you hear what Alice said?"

"I sure did." Nicholas's eyes were kind of glazed, and his goofy smile had returned.

"Will you pay attention here?" I asked. "My piano teacher drives a white van. *White. Van.* And he was trying to buy Irish cakes from an Italian baker. Why would he do that?"

"He was hungry?" Nicholas asked.

"No!" I yelled. How could Nicholas not be following this? "And you know what else? He was in a real hurry to leave here this afternoon. It all makes sense now. It was 'cause he needed to buy Irish cakes for Patrick Jamison, the *Irish* boy he kidnapped from Mayson."

Nicholas's eyes snapped back into focus. "You're right!"

"I should've known he was an alien," I said. "Humans don't have hairy spider hands. They just don't. We have to call Frank."

I reached for the phone but stopped when Dad walked in. His eyes were glazed over too, but not the same way Nicholas's had been.

"Hey, Dad," I said.

He didn't answer me. He just sat down at the table.

"Are you okay? Should I get Alice? Or call Mom?"

"Promotion," he mumbled. His eyes met mine, and the corners of his mouth rose into a smile. "I got a promotion."

CHAPTER 12
FIRED-UP DESSERT

Mom rushed through the front door just as we finished dinner. She ran straight to the kitchen without even taking off her jacket or nurse's hat. Except she didn't look excited at all. She actually looked super upset . . . kind of like the day we got the call that Grandma Esther had fallen and broken three ribs.

"I'm here! What's the big news?" she asked anxiously.

I sat back in my seat and sighed. For a split second, I'd thought maybe Grandma Esther had fallen again. Or—worse—what if Frank had gotten zapped into space on his way home?

"You sounded frantic on the phone," Mom continued. "I tried to leave work earlier, but there was a big accident on the freeway. Five ambulances arrived at the ER at the same time. I got pulled in to help and couldn't find anyone to cover for me. Terrible mess, but thank God, nothing life-threatening." She turned to Nicholas. "Is it your aunt? Is she okay?"

"She's fine, Mrs. Wexler. I mean, I guess she is. I haven't heard anything from my parents."

"Good, good." Mom rapped her knuckles on the table three times. She always did that when she was thankful or needed extra good luck. Grandma Esther did it too, but she would only do it on wood. She said it didn't count otherwise. Mom didn't seem to care, though. She had no problem knocking on the fiberglass kitchen table. Sometimes she even knocked on her own head. "So what is it?"

"You didn't tell her?" Alice asked Dad.

"It's not something you blurt out over the phone." Dad stood up and pulled out a chair for Mom. "You're going to want to sit for this."

"Howard, you're making me nervous! What is it already?" Mom looked at Dad, then glanced around at each of us, but I pinched my lips together to keep from smiling. "What's with all the odd expressions?"

"Actually," Dad said, "I changed my mind. Stand up. In fact, everyone, get up. We're going to Brusco's for dessert tonight to celebrate."

"Brusco's!" she exclaimed. "All the way in Kin-chester? Everything there is so extravagant. Why do we need to drive so far? I just got home. And why are we celebrating? What is going on?"

Dad reached out to take her hands. "Barbara, I did it. After all these years, I finally got a promotion."

Mom shrieked so loudly that the fancy dishes in the china cabinet rattled, including the collector ones we weren't allowed to touch. She threw her arms around Dad's neck. "Oh, Howie, I'm so proud of you!" Then she kissed him on the lips. Right there in front of all of us! If that wasn't bad enough, she then ran around the table and gave each of us a hug and kiss on the cheek. Even Nicholas! With each person, she repeated, "A promotion!" In case we missed the news the first time around, I guess. When she finished, she stood there shaking her head at Dad. "When? How?"

"Today, just as I was getting ready to leave," Dad started. "I was at my locker, packing up my things when Lanzo came over to me and said Carlin and Fiore wanted me to go to their office."

"Carlin and Fiore!" Mom exclaimed. "They're the big bosses."

"The biggest," Dad specified. "So of course,

I think I'm getting fired. I follow Lanzo, and I'm shaking the entire way. That office is in a part of the factory I never even knew existed . . . all fancy, with paneled walls and leather furniture. Anyway, they tell me to sit, and they start talking about the big mess from the other day with the table order, so now I think *I really am getting fired.* Except then they say they heard I saved the day, and *bam!* Next thing I know, they're giving me a promotion!"

"Wow, what a story," Mom said, still shaking her head. "This is just the most amazing news."

"That's why we need to go out and celebrate," Dad said. "Come on. We can clean up later."

I'd never been to Brusco's before. It was in Kinchester, where people could afford to buy as many sets of encyclopedias as they wanted and expensive cars too, I guess, 'cause there were a ton of them in Brusco's parking lot. There were also *no* white vans. I checked as we drove in.

In the front of the restaurant stood two huge gold lion statues, one on each side of a wide staircase. I was pretty sure they weren't made out of Dad's fiberglass. They looked way too fancy. Past the lions, the stairs led up to two gold double doors, the kind you'd expect for a mansion or a castle.

"Whoa," I said, running my hands over the lion as I walked up the stairs. Yup, definitely not fiberglass. I wondered if they were made out of real gold.

"Don't be such a dork," Alice mumbled. "And pretend you don't know me." She ran three steps ahead of all of us and lifted her head high before opening both doors together. They made a loud *swish* sound. We followed her in, but a man wearing a black tuxedo stopped us before we could get very far.

"May I help you?" he asked.

"We'd like a table," Dad proudly said. "For five."

"Do you have a reservation?"

"Oh, I didn't . . . no. Well, we're just here for dessert. We won't be very long."

The man glanced behind him into the crowded dining room. "One moment, please. Wait here."

He walked across the room to speak to another man dressed in a tuxedo and then returned. He grabbed a pile of menus and said, "Follow me, please."

As we were led to a table in the back of the room, the voices from the people already seated changed from loud chatter to hushed whispers. Several diners stopped eating to stare at us as we walked by.

"Maybe we should've changed first." Mom smoothed out her nurses' uniform as she sat.

"Nonsense," Dad said. "We're all fine." He motioned for the waiter.

"Isn't that Angela Santone?" Mom whispered.

Dad turned around for a quick peek at the table directly behind us. I turned too. I didn't recognize the lady, but if her last name was Santone, she was probably related to Mr. Santone, one of dad's bosses.

"Yes," Dad said. "Maybe I should go over and tell her to thank her husband. Jim Santone signs all the promotion slips. He must've been the one to recommend me to Carlin and Fiore."

Before Mom could respond, the waiter appeared.

"We're celebrating," Dad told him. "Kids, order any dessert you'd like. You too, Barbara," he said, giving her a kiss on the cheek. "And we'll also take two glasses of champagne."

I studied the menu. Normally I'd get chocolate cake, but this was Brusco's. *The* Brusco's. I only had one chance to get this right. I told the waiter to start with Nicholas. The decision was too important to rush. Nicholas ordered a fudge parfait with extra whipped cream, and Alice ordered the cherry cheesecake. Mom ordered a slice of cheesecake too, but she asked that hers have strawberries on top. When the waiter came back to me, I still couldn't decide.

"What's this?" I pointed to the second item on the list.

"Baked Alaska," the waiter said. "Three flavors of ice cream covered in a flaming meringue."

Flaming ice cream? Heck yeah! I nodded.

"Very well, sir," the waiter said. "I'll bring it right over."

Dad smiled and kissed the top of Mom's hand. All this kissing was grossing me out.

Nicholas twisted around to scan the room to his left. Then he scanned the room to his right.

"What are you doing?" I whispered.

"Checking for your piano teacher," he said. "Or any other sign of aliens."

Now I twisted around to scan the room too. Just 'cause I hadn't seen the white van in the parking lot didn't mean the aliens hadn't sneaked in after us.

"They'd be here if they were smart," Nicholas continued.

"Why?" I asked.

"This place is filled with rich kids. If the aliens are looking to trade, rich kids are worth more."

I was about to tell Nicholas that this maybe made sense when a voice from the table behind us suddenly distracted me.

"Jim said he ruined the entire order."

I peeked around Alice's shoulder to get a better look. It was Mr. Santone's wife. She spoke so loudly that it was impossible for us not to hear her. "He got the measurements and color all wrong. Cost his team a day's worth of overtime just to fix everything."

"Figures," a woman sitting with her replied. "Those people can't do anything right. Instead of spending his money here, he should be paying back the factory."

"You'd think, but they promoted him instead. Can you believe that? A promotion for messing up. The paperwork didn't even cross Jim's desk. He thinks it was some kind of pity promotion from the big bosses. Now that it's done, he supposes it'll be used to let certain accounts know they support their type of people."

Dad pushed his chair back with a loud screech and stood up.

"Just ignore them, Howard." Mom put her hand on his arm. "You know none of that is true."

"It's fine," he said. "We're leaving." His eyes

were stern, and he nodded toward Alice, Nicholas, and me.

"But what about dessert?" I asked.

"We're leaving. Now."

Without another word, we all stood up. The waiter approached with a tray of food, including my Baked Alaska, which really was on fire. Mom gave the poor guy a smile and said, "I'm sorry."

"But your order . . ." He steadied the tray on the palm of his hand.

Dad reached into his pocket and threw a bunch of bills on the table. "Forget it. We're not hungry anymore."

CHAPTER 13
OPERATION ALIEN HUNT

Nicholas's mom came to pick him up before breakfast on Saturday but asked if he could come back around dinnertime so that she and Nicholas's dad could head back to the hospital. It was the perfect setup, since we'd called Frank after we got back from Brusco's last night and filled him in about Mr. Schneider being an alien. Frank had promised to come over the next day with his telescope. He even remembered to ask his mom first.

Mom hardly ever ordered pizza for dinner, but tonight she surprised us with a delivery from Roma's. She even ordered a side of their famous garlic knots. I don't know if they were actually famous, but they could have been. That's how good they were. I think she felt bad that our celebration of Dad's promotion got cut short. I felt bad too, and not just 'cause I didn't get to have flaming ice cream. Anyway, Roma's pizza and world-famous garlic knots were a pretty good way to celebrate if you asked me.

"Impressive telescope you brought over, Frank," Dad said while we ate.

Last night when we got home, Dad had barely said anything, but tonight he seemed back to being excited about his big news.

"Thanks," Frank said, although it came out sounding more like a grunt since he'd shoved almost an entire piece of pizza in his mouth just as Dad started talking to him.

"It's the Spacetron Z7000. He got it for his birthday." I figured I'd help Frank out. Plus, I was worried about what might come flying out of his mouth if he tried to speak again.

"Going stargazing tonight, boys?" Mom asked.

"They're searching for UFOs so they can capture Martians and save the galaxy," Alice scoffed. "Soon our basement will be full of a bunch of little green men." She glanced over to the boxes on the counter. 'We're definitely going to need more pizza. I heard those aliens eat a lot."

"Oh, Alice," Mom said, "let the boys have their

fun. It's a nice warm night. After that awful winter we had, we could all use this early spring. The sky's nice and clear too. I'll bet you'll be able to see the Big Dipper."

"And it's a full moon," Dad added.

"Even better," Alice said with a laugh. "You can watch for werewolves too." She leaned across the table toward me and said, "I heard Mr. Schneider is one."

"That's enough, Alice," Mom warned.

"What?" she asked. "Grace Amato's brother told her he saw one once. They don't always go back to normal after the full moon goes away, you know."

Mom shook her head. "That's just some old spooky campfire story someone made up. It's not real."

"All I'm saying," Alice continued, "is that I got a real good look at Mr. Schneider's hands when he was at the bakery yesterday. Danny can tell you—he's a lot hairier than a person should be."

Dad put his slice of pizza down to examine his own hands.

"I said that's enough, Alice," said Mom sternly. "Aren't you going over to Terri's house? You're going to be late."

"Yeah," she said. "I'm going." She stood up, mouthed *"werewolf"* at me, and headed out the door.

"I thought your sister said Mr. Schneider was part spider," Frank said.

"I thought he was an alien," Nicholas added.

Mom glared at us.

"We should set up outside," I said, standing up. "It's starting to get dark out."

"Stay in the backyard, take your sweatshirts, and don't go any farther than the fence," Mom told us. "And be in by nine-thirty."

Out in the living room, we grabbed Frank's telescope and some other supplies I'd thrown in my backpack earlier, including my Super-Secret Spy Notebook. I'd never shown it to anyone, not even Frank, but since we were all in this together, it seemed like a good time.

"The last thing I need to be worrying about is them wandering around in the dark with a kidnapper on the loose." Mom's voice trailed out of the kitchen.

"Oh, they'll be fine, Barbara," Dad responded. "They'll only be a few feet away."

"We're all set." I walked back into the kitchen with Nicholas and Frank.

"Here." Mom handed us a couple of flashlights and a bag that held the rest of the garlic knots. "The aliens might be hungry."

"Thanks."

"Listen," Dad said, taking the bag out of my hands and pulling two knots out for himself before giving it back to me. "Keep those Martians outside, you hear? I don't want to have to clean green slime out of the basement."

"Got it," I said. We headed out the back door with our supplies.

Frank picked a spot clear of the trees and set up the telescope while I grabbed three chairs from the patio.

"You know, it kind of makes sense," Nicholas said.

"What makes sense?" I asked.

"What your sister said. That Mr. Schneider is part werewolf."

"You think everything my sister says makes sense," I told him. "I thought we already decided he was an alien."

"He could be both," Frank said. "And it would explain a lot."

"What do you mean?"

"Well," Frank went on, "it's like your sister was saying—Mr. Schneider is super hairy on his arms and hands. Maybe on his legs too."

"Ew," I said.

"And I get where the spider thing comes from,

especially with those bulging eyes, but the hair on his hands is definitely more like fur than spidery fuzz. Plus, spiders have eight legs. So I think we can cross that one off of the list. Besides, I thought his teeth were a little fanglike when he was talking to us the other day."

"Yeah," Nicholas agreed, "I noticed that too."

"Wouldn't that make him a vampire?" I asked.

"No, not vampire fangs, wolf-type fangs," Nicholas explained. "And his voice got kind of growly when he told us to go to the kitchen."

"So where does the alien part come in? You said he could be both." I took a seat in the chair farthest from the bushes that lined our backyard. If Mr. Schneider *was* part werewolf, he'd probably want to hide out in woods. And since we didn't have any woods, he'd have to use our bushes.

"Well, he can't switch back to human," Frank explained, "because he *isn't* human. He's alien. So a guy that appears kind of human but still has extrahairy hands is the best the Martians could come up with, I guess."

"Yeah, okay." I pulled my book out of my backpack.

"What's that?" Frank asked.

"My Super-Secret Spy Notebook. We can use it to keep track of clues, but you have to swear that whatever we write in here stays between us. Deal?"

Frank and Nicholas nodded. Then we all put our hands on top of the book.

"Swear," we all said together.

I started to turn to my *Unsolved Mysteries* page but decided this investigation was important enough for a space of its own. I opened to an empty page and started writing.

Operation Alien Hunt

Facts:

1. *Missing boats & planes from Bermuda Triangle were zapped by UFOs.*

2. *The kid from Mayson was kidnapped by White Van Guy.*

3. *The white van with the kidnapped kid was zapped by the Bermuda Triangle UFO.*

4. *Mr. Schneider drives a white van and is a werewolf alien.*

5. *Missing Mayson kid is being held on a faraway planet with missing Bermuda Triangle boats and planes.*

6. *Mr. Schneider IS A WEREWOLF WHITE VAN BERMUDA TRIANGLE ALIEN KIDNAPPER!!!*

Seeing the words on paper made it feel a thousand times more real. I glanced sideways at the bushes again and made sure my flashlight was on its brightest setting. "Anything else?"

"The reward?" Nicholas said.

"Right."

7. *$2,000 reward for leads!*

"That's pretty much it," Frank said. His voice sounded a little shaky as his eyes darted upward. "Guess we'd better have a look through the telescope. I'll go first."

He walked over to the telescope to see if he could find any proof of werewolf white van Bermuda Triangle alien UFOs in the sky.

CHAPTER 14
UNEXPECTED SIGHTINGS

While Frank peered through the telescope, Nicholas and I stayed in our chairs, shining our flashlights on each corner of the backyard to keep watch for werewolves.

"Sure is dark out here," I said. "Even with that full moon. Maybe I should go ask Dad to turn on the patio light."

"I won't be able to see as well," Frank said. "And keep those flashlights still, will you? Every time I see a light bouncing off of the grass, I think it's coming from a UFO up there."

"Well, what are we supposed to do, then?" Nicholas asked. "Just sitting around is boring."

Frank picked up the Super-Secret Spy Notebook off of my lap and turned to the next blank page.

"Here," he said, handing it to Nicholas. "Make a map of the sky for us to use. Like a grid or something. That way we can keep track of any spots that seem suspicious. Right now I'm focusing on that top left corner." He pointed to an area of the sky that was more toward the back of the yard, although wasn't the entire sky *the top*? "When we switch, you'll take top middle, and then Danny can scan top right. Then we'll move to the middle section of the sky. Make sense?"

"You've put a lot of thought into this," Nicholas said.

"You can't catch aliens without a plan," I pointed out.

Frank nodded.

"Yeah, okay," Nicholas agreed.

I shined my flashlight on the notebook while Nicholas drew the grid. It kind of reminded me of a tic-tac-toe game. He drew an *X* in the top left square.

At first, I thought Nicholas was marking off the spot where Frank had his telescope pointed so we'd know he had that part of the sky covered. But then he handed the notebook and pencil to me. Nicholas was right—it *was* boring just sitting here. So I drew an *O* in the bottom right square. Nicholas totally fell for it and put his next X directly under his first one. I made my move, putting an O in the bottom left square.

Frank turned around just as Nicholas was about to mark his next X. "What are you two doing?" He seemed pretty annoyed.

"I told you," Nicholas said. "We're bored."

"Fine." Frank grabbed the notebook out of my hands and stood next to Nicholas's chair. He drew a second grid and put a giant check mark in one of the boxes. "Top left is all clear. Go ahead and scope out top middle."

"Finally," Nicholas said. He jumped up and walked over to the telescope. "Whoa, you can see everything! Stars and planets and the moon and— hey, I see something moving. I really do!"

Frank threw my Super-Secret Spy Notebook into my lap and ran over. I ran over too, but I held the book close to my chest. It wasn't something you could just throw around.

"Let me see!" Frank shouted and shoved Nicholas over.

"Hey," Nicholas yelled. "It's my turn! You're just supposed to mark it off on the grid, remember?"

Frank ignored him and looked through the

telescope. "I don't see anything," he said. "And you're not even pointed at top middle. We had a plan."

"You mean you had a plan," Nicholas said. "Anyway, it's a good thing I wasn't only on top middle 'cause I would've missed it."

"Missed what?" Frank snapped. "Your made-up spaceship?"

"It wasn't made up!" Nicholas's voice grew louder and angrier. "It was there. It was round and had lights all around that spun as it moved."

"Let me see!" I demanded. I put the notebook carefully on the chair. "I haven't even had a turn yet."

Frank moved to the side. "Go ahead. But there's nothing there." He scowled at Nicholas and repeated, "Nothing."

"I know what I saw!" Nicholas yelled. "It was going like a million miles an hour—that's why it was gone so fast." He took a step closer to Frank and clenched his fists by his side. "You're just mad 'cause you didn't see it first. You have to catch it at exactly the right millisecond." He stood up straight and puffed out his chest. "And I did."

Frank tightened his fists too.

"Cut it out!" I pushed my body between the two of them.

Before either of them could make another move, the patio light went on, and the back door opened. Frank and Nicholas backed away from each other.

"Snacks, anyone?" Mom walked out carrying a tray and placed it on the small patio table. "Can't be on an alien watch without popcorn. And I brought you hot cocoa too. It's starting to get a little chilly out here."

"Thanks, Mrs. Wexler." Frank walked over to where she stood.

"Yeah, thanks." Nicholas followed, his voice now back to normal.

"See anything good?" Mom asked.

"Maybe," I answered, hoping Nicholas and Frank wouldn't start fighting again.

They didn't say a word.

"Well," she said, taking her tray back after putting the bowls and cups on the table, "I won't keep you from your fun." She walked back inside.

"Let's say that was a spaceship," Frank began. He shoveled popcorn in his mouth and took a big gulp of hot chocolate without even testing it first to make sure it wasn't too hot.

"It was a spaceship," Nicholas insisted.

"That's what I said." Frank tossed another handful

of popcorn in his mouth and kept talking. "What if it was staking out the area but saw the light from the flashlights, knew someone was watching for it, and set its engine to supersonic turbo so it could vanish faster than a blink of an eye? That could explain why only Nicholas saw it."

"Exactly." Nicholas threw a huge handful of popcorn in his mouth too. "A million miles an hour, just like I said."

"But why was it over my backyard?" I scanned the area nervously. "Is it 'cause Mr. Schneider told them about me, and they're planning on taking me next?" I knew I should have been nicer to him. "M-maybe we should go inside."

"Nah," Frank said. "Mr. Schneider's already had plenty of chances to grab you. No offense, but I don't think he's interested."

In a strange way, I *was* kind of offended. I also wasn't 100 percent certain that I believed Frank.

"Actually, I think the UFO was out searching for Mr. Schneider," Nicholas said. "You know, so it could zap him back up."

"Yeah, you're probably right," Frank agreed. "I'll bet he's still out here somewhere 'cause he was trying to find food for that Irish kid. Except now the spaceship is gone, so Mr. Schneider is stuck here, hanging around."

I brought my Super-Secret Spy Notebook over to the table.

8. Mr. Schneider needs to get back on UFO.

"And there's a full moon," Nicholas said, his eyes rising toward the sky. "I wonder . . ."

"What do you wonder?" I already knew, but I was hoping he was going to say something *other* than that Mr. Schneider had turned into a full werewolf.

"I wonder if . . ." He stopped talking because the bushes along the side of the house began to rustle. We all looked over. I held my breath.

"Probably a squirrel," Frank whispered.

The bushes shook again. That was either a huge family of squirrels or a single giant one. I reached for one of the flashlights but realized they were all still next to the chairs out by the telescope. I squinted, trying to see across the dark yard. The rustling stopped. And I let out my breath.

"Anyway," Frank continued, "if the spaceship *was* searching for Mr. Schneider, maybe it'll come back. Let's finish our stakeout." He headed back to the middle of the yard where our chairs and telescope were set up. Nicholas and I stayed close behind him.

"*ROARRRRR!*" From out of the bushes hurtled a body—humanlike with legs and arms, wearing a dark coat, but with the head of a wolf—furry with red eyes and pointy teeth. Behind it, another body, also in a dark coat—this one with a green head, four huge bloody eyeballs, and long silver antennae. They waved their arms as they ran around the yard screaming.

Nicholas, Frank, and I screamed too, nearly knocking each other over as we raced to get to the back door. I didn't even have time to grab my Super-Secret Spy Notebook, which broke the most important rule of being a Super-Secret spy.

All the backyard lights came on. Dad swung the door open. "What is going on out here?" he yelled.

"It's Mr. Schneider!" I cried. "He's here with one of the other aliens! Quick, let us in!"

I tried to push through the doorway, but Dad just stood there blocking my path. He shook his head and seemed totally annoyed. Behind me, the sound of familiar laughter erupted. I spun around. Alice stood doubled over with her friend Terri, the two of them cackling. In Alice's hand was a rubber wolf mask, and in Terri's, a green rubber Martian mask.

"That wasn't funny!" I screamed.

"Oh, it really is," Alice said, barely able to catch her breath.

"No, it isn't." Mom now stood in the doorway too, arms crossed. She seemed annoyed like Dad, but she also looked like she might cry. "I nearly called 9-1-1." She turned to Alice's friend. "Terri, does your mom know you're here?"

"No, Mrs. Wexler." She kept her head low. "I'm sorry."

"It's not me you should be apologizing to."

Normally, I'd kill for an apology from Alice and Terri, but my heart was beating so loudly that I couldn't even hear their words.

Mom made Terri leave and sent Alice to her room. Then she turned to us. "Maybe it's time to wrap up the stargazing for tonight, boys. Why don't you bring everything inside? You can watch television until it's time for bed."

She didn't have to ask me twice. And I was glad she left all the lights on out back until we were done. I'd had enough white-van-werewolf-Bermuda-Triangle-UFO-alien hunting for one night.

CHAPTER 15
TROUBLES

As I got ready for school on Monday, I counted five door slams, all from my sister: once when she entered the bathroom, once when she went back into her bedroom, twice from the door to her closet, and a final slam as she left the house. That one made everything inside shake, even the fancy dishes. I was pretty sure it was 'cause she'd been grounded for an entire month, which included our upcoming week of spring break. Not that I dared to ask her. Regular Alice was bad enough. I didn't want to go anywhere near raging Alice.

On my way to school, I was so preoccupied with watching for the white van that I bumped straight into two light poles and a phone booth. I even nearly knocked over old Mr. Vernon as he came out of his house, but Frank called my name and stopped me.

"We need a new plan," Frank told me as we walked up to the school.

Nicholas wasn't waiting for us at the front of the building, which was strange 'cause he'd said he'd meet Frank and me on the outside steps first thing today.

"You don't think we should keep watching for . . ." I wanted to say more, but there were too many kids walking past, so I just said, "You don't think we should keep looking through your telescope?"

"Oh, we definitely should keep doing that. Especially since Nicholas saw—you know."

The bell rang, which meant we only had three minutes to get to class. I scanned the area one more time for Nicholas and then headed inside with Frank. Maybe Nicholas's bus was late today.

"But the . . ." I glanced over my shoulder and whispered, "UFO," before continuing in my normal voice. "It was going so fast. It's not like we could do anything. We wouldn't even be able to take a picture if we saw it again."

Once inside Mrs. Greely's classroom, everyone stopped talking to watch me. Well, not Nicholas.

Guess his bus wasn't late after all. There he was, already at his desk, staring straight ahead.

I walked over to him. "Hey," I said. "I thought you were meeting us outside."

He kept his eyes forward and shrugged. The bell to start school rang before I could ask him more.

The morning dragged. First, Mrs. Greely handed back our English essays from last week. Our topic had been to write about something adventurous we wanted to try. Mrs. Greely asked for a volunteer to read their essay out loud, and Eugene Barone raised his hand. He was always raising his hand for stuff like that. His essay was about going on one of those big cruise ships one day because he'd never been on a boat before. It didn't sound all that adventurous to me, but then he mentioned a bunch of islands this boat might visit, and one of them was Bermuda. I thought about warning him about the Bermuda Triangle, but since the essay was about doing something adventurous, I didn't. Plus, Frank, Nicholas, and I were pretty sure the aliens weren't there anymore anyway.

For math, we had to find the area of shapes that weren't even real shapes. They were weirdly connected lines and curves. I began to think that somewhere out there was a nerdy, mean person who had the job of making up those awful non-shapes just to torture us kids in math class.

Halfway through the lesson, Bobby Caldon let out the loudest fart ever. Everyone burst out laughing. Everyone except Nicholas. He still had a scowl on his face. I tore a small corner piece of paper from my notebook and scribbled:

What's the matter? You get in trouble or something?

Then I folded it up and slid it over to him with my foot. I had to get out of my seat a tiny bit to reach him but quickly sat back down.

He didn't notice. Mrs. Greely did.

She walked over, picked up the note, and slipped it in her pocket. Then she walked to the chalkboard and drew another weird diagram on the board. This one was even more non-shapey than the others, if you can believe that.

"Daniel," she said, holding up her chalk. She didn't say anything more. We all knew that when Mrs. Greely called your name and held out her chalk, it meant you were supposed to go to the board and solve the problem in front of the class. After a few minutes and lots of erasing, she told me to keep working while the rest of the class got to start their homework. Just as I finally came up with an answer, the bell rang for recess. I expected Mrs. Greely to call me over for a lecture, but instead, she nodded. So I ran outside with everyone else.

I stood next to Nicholas, expecting him to pick me for kickball as usual, but he didn't. He picked Eugene. No one ever picked Eugene—not 'cause he wasn't any good but 'cause he never wanted to play. He liked to hang out by the slide where it wasn't so crowded, which was exactly where he was when Nicholas picked his team. Bobby had to run all the way over there to grab him.

"What gives?" I asked when I was the only one who hadn't been picked.

"No more spots," Nicholas said.

I followed him as he walked over to take his place in the outfield.

"But you always give me a spot." I wanted to be angry, but really, I was just confused.

"Maybe I felt like giving it to someone else."

"You can have mine." Frank walked toward us from his position at first base. "I'll hang by the side-lines and keep score."

"Well, if Frank's not playing, I'm not playing either," Nicholas said, and he walked off the kickball field, leaving Frank and me standing there.

"Hey!" I yelled, running after him. "What's the matter with you? You mad at me or something? There wasn't anything bad in that note Mrs. Greely picked up, I swear."

Nicholas spun around. He had the same serious expression he'd had on Saturday night when he was arguing with Frank about seeing the spaceship. His hands were even clenched into fists too.

"Just leave me alone," he growled.

"What? Why?"

He stepped so close to me that I could feel his warm breath on my face. "I said leave me alone. I can't talk to you anymore."

I knew I should walk away, but I also knew I hadn't done anything wrong. "Why can't you talk to me?"

His eyes grew scary-wide, but they also seemed kind of sad. "Because my mom and dad said so." Then he turned and walked back to the kickball game, leaving me standing all alone.

CHAPTER 16
BACKYARD GIRLS CLUB

I snuck out of my seat again to pass Nicholas another note during social studies. He pretended not to notice it was right there on the floor next to his feet, even though I knew he saw it. Since I didn't want to get either of us in trouble, I slipped out of my seat for the third time that day to take it back. At our second recess, I walked straight up to him before he even had a chance to start picking his team for kickball.

"I want to know what's going on," I demanded. "Why don't your parents want you talking to me anymore?"

Nicholas wouldn't answer. He also refused to look at me. He just stood there and dug the toe of his sneaker into the blacktop, trying to loosen a pebble.

"Okay, fine," I said. "At least tell me why you're going around telling other people to be mean to me."

"I'm not doing that," he responded, finally lifting his head.

"Then why is everybody staring and whispering? And how come Bobby and Vincent didn't eat lunch with Frank and me like they always do?"

"Ask Bobby and Vincent." He tried to walk around me, but I moved to the side with him, blocking his path.

"Come on, Nicholas," I said. "Tell me what's going on."

Joey Simone, the biggest kid in the sixth grade, stepped between us so that he was face-to-face with me—although not quite, since I only came up to his neck.

"We're done putting up with you," Joey said. "That's what's going on."

He pushed on my shoulders, and I knew he wanted me to push him back. But this was Joey Simone. He'd totally beat me up. I'd either get in trouble for fighting and be grounded for a month with Alice, or I'd be dead. Neither one of those things sounded fun. I tried to keep my knees from shaking as I took a step back. "What's that supposed to mean?" I asked, wishing my voice wasn't shaking too.

"It means you should go live in Larston where you belong."

Frank grabbed my elbow and pulled me out of the growing crowd before I could say anything more. "Come on," he said. "Let's go." He dragged me all the way to the rusted monkey bars on the side of the school where no one would see us.

"Why would he say something like that?" I asked as we climbed to the top. "Do you think he found out about what happened on Saturday night? Is that why everyone's acting weird? Is that why Nicholas's parents say he can't talk to me anymore? People get funny when you start talking about aliens and UFOs, you know?"

"It has nothing to do with that." Frank swung his legs through the bars, together at first, then alternating right and left. "I heard my dad on the phone last night. Some of the guys down at the factory have been talking."

"About what?"

"About your dad's . . ." He stopped.

All the nasty words those ladies at Brusco's had said came rushing back. *Pity promotion. Those people can't do anything right.* "The promotion?" I asked. "The guys in the factory don't think he deserved it either?"

Frank shook his head.

"So their kids are mad too?" I asked. "But my dad worked hard for that promotion."

"I know, and that's what my dad told them," Frank said. "Those other guys are just being stupid."

"It doesn't make sense to me," I said. "And I'll tell you what else—it's not fair." I swung my legs in the exact same alternating pattern as Frank. "It's just not fair," I repeated.

After school, I stopped at Mrs. Albertini's house. A lot had happened since I'd seen her last. She had on the same flower-print dress that she always wore and took me straight to the kitchen. I ate an entire slice of Scholly's chocolate-frosted pound cake before I even said a word.

"Have you ever been to Larston?" I asked.

"Not for years." She put her kettle on the stove for tea. "When I was a girl, my mother and I would go every week. There used to be a shop on Sandy Mill Road that was owned by a sweet old couple. My mother said they made the best borscht she'd ever tasted. Made me promise to never tell my bubbe."

"Why not?" I asked. "And what's borscht?"

"Oh, it's a wonderful soup made from beets. But my bubbe thought she made the best borscht, and you didn't argue with Bubbe. You just didn't. It was a long drive, but every Wednesday after school, my mother and I would head to Larston. First, we'd visit my Aunt Ida. Then we'd check in on the rabbi's wife, Mrs. Cassewitz. She always smelled like cinnamon and roses. From there, we'd go see Mr. Haber, the kosher butcher. My mother had to examine every cut of meat before he had permission to wrap it up. And finally, we'd pick up some of my mother's favorite borscht." Mrs. Albertini smiled. "I miss those days."

"So you didn't grow up there?"

"No." Mrs. Albertini shook her head. "I grew up on the other side of the river in Oxly. My father wanted to live in Larston, but he had to travel to the city three days a week for work. We needed to live closer to the train station. Why all the questions?"

"Some kids at school said I don't belong in Croyfield. They said I belong in Larston. I'm pretty sure it's 'cause that's where all the Jewish kids live."

Mrs. Albertini sighed and poured her tea. "People can be cruel. I don't want you to pay any attention to them. You have as much right to be here as they do. Understand?"

I nodded, but it didn't make anything better. Not really.

"Honestly," she continued, "all these years and nothing has changed. Not a darn thing."

"This happened when you were a kid too?" I asked.

"Oxly was no different. I was called names I don't dare repeat to you. My entire family was. Don't get me wrong—not everyone was mean. Just like not everyone at your school is mean. But there were enough. More than enough. I was lucky to have a couple of good friends, Sally and Marge, who liked me for me. In fact, it was my friend Sally who introduced me to Mr. Albertini." She nodded at his photo on the shelf over the sink.

"At least your friends were allowed to hang out with you," I said. "My friend Nicholas—well, I guess he's my ex-friend now. His parents told him that they don't want him around me anymore."

Mrs. Albertini lifted her eyes from the picture of her husband. "Sally's parents told her the same thing. They didn't like us, and they didn't want their daughter around me."

"So how did you stay friends?"

Mrs. Albertini's attention went back to the photo.

"Sally, Marge, and I used to meet in Marge's backyard. It was surrounded by rows of tall trees, and we knew we could sneak back there without Sally's parents knowing. Marge's dad even built us a little clubhouse in the back corner. We hung a sign over the door that said BGC . . . Backyard Girls Club. Why, you might be the only one outside of the BGC and Mr. Albertini whom I've ever told about it."

"We hang out in my backyard. Frank and me, I mean. And Nicholas, before . . . you know."

Mrs. Albertini smiled but seemed stuck on her memories. "I'll never forget that day in April when Sally was invited to a school dance here in Croyfield. Her date asked that she bring someone along for his buddy. Marge was out of town, so I got to go. I had to get my own ride and pretend I wasn't with Sally, of course, since her parents didn't know we were still friends. But it was worth it. My mystery date turned out to be none other than Gino Albertini."

"Neat." I didn't mean to sound uninterested, but when stories took a turn for the mushy, I sort of zoned out.

"I should be getting home," I said, pushing my chair back. "Thanks for the cake."

"I'm glad you stopped by," Mrs. Albertini said.

When she said that, I remembered the *actual* reason I had stopped by. "I almost forgot to tell you—my dad got a promotion."

"Did he? I'm so glad. Please congratulate him for me."

She smiled but didn't seem as excited as I'd expected.

"I will. Thanks," I said before heading out the door.

I'd just about reached my front steps when I felt a hand grasp my shoulder.

CHAPTER 17
SNEAKING AROUND

I froze. I wanted to run, but instead, I kept perfectly still. Was the white van nearby? I'd been extra careful to check for it lately whenever I walked outside. Especially when I walked alone. But I'd been distracted by my talk with Mrs. Albertini. My eyes slowly slid sideways to get a glimpse of the hand resting on my shoulder. *Please don't let it be hairy.*

It wasn't. It was a kid's hand, about the size of my own. I spun around.

"Nicholas?" I could barely hear my voice over my pounding heart.

He wore a black sweatshirt with the hood up over his head so that it covered most of his face.

"Not so loud," he whispered. "My mom will kill me if she sees me here. I'm supposed to be at the market getting tomatoes." He checked over his shoulders and then pulled his hood even farther over his face. "So can I come in or what?"

I wasn't in the mood to hear him tell me all over again how he didn't want to be my friend anymore. He was probably only interested in seeing Alice anyway. But I couldn't get Mrs. Albertini's friend Sally out of my head. "Yeah, okay," I said.

Inside, Nicholas headed straight through to the kitchen, opened the door to the patio, and walked back outside. Without even asking or anything.

"Did you leave something out here the other night?" I asked.

He sat on the edge of the patio and pushed his hood off his head, staring up at the sky as he spoke. "I didn't know Joey was going to say that today. The stuff about Larston. It's not what I think."

I sat down next to him but didn't say anything.

"My dad . . . he said he was on the list for the next round of promotions with a bunch of other people. But then his boss told them they lost money from an order that got messed up. Said promotions wouldn't happen. Made it sound like some of them might even get fired 'cause of it. Made it sound like your dad made the mistake."

"He didn't make any mistake," I told him. "He just told the bosses about it. Before it became a bigger mistake. That's why he got the promotion."

"Some people are upset about it, that's all."

I reached down and picked at a weed that was growing between the cracks of the patio. "So they're mad because my dad got a promotion and they didn't? And that makes it okay to say awful stuff about my family?" I forced myself to look Nicholas in the eye. "My dad never got promotions when everyone else did, including your dad." I stood up. My voice was getting angrier. "And you know what else? Every time that happened, I still stayed friends with you. I never said nasty things to the other kids."

"I know that," Nicholas said. "That's why I'm here. I feel bad about it all. And I swear I didn't say nasty things about you to anyone. I'm just . . ." He glanced over his shoulder again. "I'm just sorry, okay?"

I took a breath to calm myself and sat back down. "Okay."

Neither one of us said anything else. We just sat— me picking at weeds, Nicholas watching the sky.

"There's still no info on that missing kid," Nicholas said eventually. "I heard they even bumped up the reward to three thousand."

"Wow. That's a lot of money. A thousand for each of us." I thought about everything I could buy with a thousand dollars. I'd definitely get a new bicycle since mine was super old and not very fast, and maybe I'd get a set of encyclopedias too.

"So that means I'm still in?" He finally turned to me. "I can still come over to search for aliens and UFOs with you and Frank?"

"What about your parents?" I asked.

He smirked. "They don't have to know."

"Right," I agreed.

"I should probably get going." Nicholas stood and headed back into the kitchen.

Mom entered the same time we did. "I was just about to come get you, Danny," she said. "Mr. Schneider is here. Hello, Nicholas. How's your aunt?"

Nicholas's face turned white. I didn't know what color my face was, but I had a pretty good idea it had turned as white as his.

"S—she's fine," Nicholas replied.

"What's Mr. Schneider doing here?" I blurted. "It's not Friday!" I walked over to the doorway to peek into the living room. Sure enough, there he was, staring out the front window. His hands were clasped behind his back and looked hairier than ever.

"He called me and said you were a bit uncooperative on Friday." Mom briefly glanced at Nicholas before returning to me. "We can talk about that later. He asked to make up your lesson today."

"But I haven't practiced," I protested.

"All the more reason you need a lesson," Mom said. "Come on. Let's not keep him waiting. And this time, show a little respect, please. He rearranged his entire schedule to come over today."

"I'll bet," I mumbled. What with snatching kids into the white van, transforming back and forth between alien werewolf and a human spider, and flying around the universe, he probably didn't have a lot of free time. "Hey, can Nicholas stay around?" I asked. I turned to Nicholas. "You'll be quiet, won't you?"

"Yeah," Nicholas said. He leaned over and whispered in my ear, "What about the tomatoes? I'm supposed to be at the market, remember?"

I reached into the fridge, grabbed two from the vegetable drawer, and handed them to him. Then I smiled at Mom. "It's okay, right? His mom asked if he could borrow a couple."

She furrowed her brow. "Just go out there and behave, please."

Nicholas took the tomatoes and followed me out to the living room.

"Mr. Schneider?" He had his back to me, and I braced myself. We'd just had that full moon, and Alice's friend said sometimes werewolves didn't always switch all the way back to human—or whatever the heck he was. He could be some weird combo of werewolf, spider, and alien right now.

He slowly turned, and I let out a sigh of relief. He'd morphed back into human . . . or at least his version of a hairy-handed, bald, bug-eyed human.

"Daniel," he said with a weird nod. He did one of those sideways eye glares at Nicholas but didn't say hello or anything. Then he took a seat at the piano and began playing the part of Beethoven's *Ode to Joy* that he had started to teach me last week. His hairy fingers scurried along the keys as usual. With Mom in the kitchen and Nicholas on the couch, I figured Mr. Schneider wouldn't zap me up into his spaceship. At least, I hoped he wouldn't. It wasn't like anyone could have stopped him.

Mr. Schneider finished playing, and Nicholas stood right next to the piano, watching.

"Can I help you?" Mr. Schneider asked him.

"I'm okay," Nicholas said. "Hey, did you ever find your Irish tart?"

I frowned across the piano at him. Why would he ask something like that? I wanted to kick Nicholas, but I was sitting on the other side of Mr. Schneider, so instead, I wiggled my eyebrows to try to get his attention. He didn't seem to notice.

"Excuse me?" Mr. Schneider said.

"The Irish tart," Nicholas repeated, calm as could be. "Danny's sister saw you in Scholly's on Friday after you left here. I was just wondering because it sounded good. I thought maybe you could tell me where to find one."

"No," Mr. Schneider answered. Then he pointed to the keys for me to play.

"You know, they might have something like that at a bakery where you live," Nicholas interrupted. "You're not from Croyfield, right? I've never seen you around here before. Other than for Danny's piano lesson."

"Can we get back to Beethoven, Daniel?" Mr. Schneider asked, ignoring Nicholas. I began playing *Ode to Joy* again but fumbled right as I got to the end of my part.

"I hear that kid from Mayson is still missing,"

Nicholas continued as if I weren't in the middle of a piano lesson with a white-van-driving Bermuda Triangle alien werewolf kidnapper.

Mr. Schneider sighed loudly.

"Everything okay in here?" Mom popped her head in from the kitchen.

Mr. Schneider glanced at Nicholas and then glanced at Mom.

"Your mom's waiting on those tomatoes, isn't she, Nicholas?" she asked.

"Yeah, I guess. Thanks, Mrs. Wexler. See ya, Danny." He stopped right before he got to the front door. "Where did you say you lived again, Mr. Schneider?" he asked.

"Goodbye, Nicholas," Mom said, and she shut the door behind him.

Mr. Schneider turned back to me and opened his mouth to speak. This time, I was almost positive I saw them—alien werewolf fangs.

CHAPTER 18
SUPER-SECRET MARTIAN CODE

The next morning, I woke up to rain. Mom insisted on driving me to school. Something about lots of sick kids in the ER lately and not wanting me to sit in wet socks all day. If you asked me, though, she was less worried about wet socks and more worried about the kidnapper. Last night's news report had said that the kid from Mayson was still missing and that there were no clues about White Van Guy. But when I mentioned to her that Mr. Schneider drove a white van, she told me I was being ridiculous. It made no sense to me.

Since we had to take Alice to her school first and she always took *forever* getting ready in the morning, I barely made it to my seat before the bell rang. Frank and Nicholas were already there, and like yesterday, the other kids stared and snickered when I walked in. At least Nicholas didn't seem miserable anymore.

We had indoor recess because of the rain, so Mrs. Greely pulled out a bunch of board games and other activities. She told us we could push our desks together as long as we kept our voices down. Frank slid his right over to mine, but Nicholas didn't move.

"Over here," Bobby Caldon called to him from the other side of the room.

Bobby, Joey, and Vincent all huddled around their pushed-together desks. Nicholas glanced at Frank and me but then joined them.

I was steamed. Had he forgotten yesterday and all that stuff he'd said about being sorry? I'd even given him two tomatoes!

I was just about to go over and tell him all that when Mrs. Albertini's friend Sally popped into my head, and I realized maybe they'd had to pretend not to be friends at school too.

"You hear about the kid in Oxly?" Frank asked, pulling me out of my thoughts.

"What kid in Oxly?"

"Some girl says she was walking to her bus stop yesterday morning when a white van pulled up next to her."

"Did the driver have really hairy hands?" I asked.

"Don't know," he said. "She ran away before anything happened. Nobody else saw anything."

"That's how it always is." I sat back in my chair.

The voices from the boys sitting across the room grew louder.

"You take that back!" Nicholas yelled.

"So now you're defending Matzah Boy?" Joey Simone asked.

"Maybe I am," Nicholas said.

"You're making a big mistake, Russo," Joey warned.

Nicholas stood up. "You're the one making a mistake." Then he pushed his desk back across the room toward Frank and me.

He sat down with us as if nothing had just happened.

Mrs. Greely, who had stepped out to make copies of a math worksheet for after recess, came rushing in.

"What is going on in here?" she demanded. "I can hear shouting all the way down the hallway. Do you need something to keep you quiet?" She held up the stack of papers in her hand.

The chatter in the room went back to its normal hushed tones.

"Thanks," I told Nicholas. "You didn't have to do that."

"They're just a bunch of jerks anyway," he said. "Hey, did you tell Frank about Mr. Schneider coming to your house yesterday?"

"What?"

I could tell Frank was shocked because the word came out half-whisper, half-squeal. Heavy on the squeal. Mrs. Greely cleared her throat toward our direction.

"Why was he at your house?" Frank asked, his voice back to a normal whisper.

I shook my head. "My mom set up a make-up piano lesson. Because I never really had one on Friday."

"How did it go? Did he do anything suspicious?"

"No," I answered. "It was just a stupid, boring lesson."

"You're wrong," Nicholas said. "A lot happened."

"What do you mean?" I asked.

"I was watching," he replied.

"You weren't watching," I told him. "You were doing a whole lot of talking. Mr. Schneider didn't like it one bit. When you left, Mr. Schneider snarled, and I actually saw his fangs. They're real, just like you said."

"Whoa," Frank mumbled.

"Yeah," I continued. "He wasn't happy about all the interruptions."

"I was trying to get some information out of him," Nicholas said. "And I was trying to distract him so he wouldn't catch on to me."

"Catch on to you doing what?" Frank asked. "Would someone please tell me what's going on?"

Nicholas leaned across his desk, and Frank and I leaned in too. "I think Mr. Schneider was trying to send a message back to his spaceship through the piano."

"What do you mean?" None of that made any sense to me.

"You thought I was standing there asking questions, but I wasn't. I was paying attention, and there was a pattern in the way he played the notes," Nicholas explained.

I sat back up straight and rolled my eyes. "He was playing Beethoven. Unless . . ." I leaned back in. "That's it! Beethoven must be their leader." I cracked up laughing. But then I stopped 'cause Nicholas wasn't laughing—and 'cause he'd just stood up for me with those other boys. "Sorry," I murmured. "Keep going."

"I'm not talking about Beethoven," Nicholas said.

"What are you talking about?" Frank asked.

"I'm talking about what he did in between playing the song. You didn't notice, Danny, but I did. In between playing Beethoven, he kept hitting notes that weren't part of the piece. It was definitely a code."

"Okay, so let's say it was a code," I said. "What does it all mean?"

"That's the part we need to figure out," Nicholas said.

"Maybe he was trying to tell the spaceship he didn't get the girl in Oxly," Frank offered.

"What girl in Oxly?" Nicholas asked.

"You didn't hear about it either?"

"No."

Frank spent the next few minutes filling Nicholas in. After that, Joey and Vincent started getting loud again, and Mrs. Greely decided recess was over.

By the time our second recess rolled around, the rain had stopped. We ran outside, but when Nicholas tried to take his place next to Bobby as kickball team captain, Joey pushed him out of the way.

"Hey," Nicholas yelled. "What do you think you're doing? I'm team captain."

"Not anymore," Joey said. "I want to be captain now."

"But it's still my turn," Nicholas said. He shoved Joey away and tried to step into the captain's spot, but Joey was too quick and pushed him back.

Mrs. Greely rushed over. "Boys!" she yelled. "Stop this right now!"

"But I'm team captain, and then Joey comes along and says *he's* team captain!"

"Why does he always get to be captain?" Joey asked.

"Because I won Rock, Paper, Scissors, remember? I get to be captain for the whole month."

"But you won last month too. Why can't someone else have a turn?" Joey complained.

Mrs. Greely sighed. "Neither of you will be captain today." She pointed to Vincent. "Here's your new captain. Now both of you behave."

She walked back over to her spot on the stairs.

Joey mumbled something not nice under his breath and walked away, while Nicholas, Frank, and I waited to be picked on a team. We weren't.

"It's just a stupid game anyway," Nicholas said, but I could tell he was pretty upset.

"Sorry," I told him, 'cause I knew the whole thing was because of me.

We walked over to the swings.

"You know, I was thinking." I took the swing in the middle. "Yesterday, Mr. Schneider kept looking out the window, but not toward the street. He was looking up at the sky."

"Because of the message he was sending," Nicholas said.

"So what's our next step?" Frank asked. "Do you think we should tell someone?"

"Not yet," Nicholas said. "First, we have to know what he's saying to . . ." He stopped talking and checked to make sure no one was nearby. "The Martians."

"And how are we going to do that?" Frank asked. "You speak Martian?"

"I do," I said.

Frank and Nicholas both raised their eyebrows at me.

"I mean, I bet I could learn. My Super-Secret Spy Notebook came with a book that teaches you how to break codes. In the back, there's a whole section with a bunch of cryptic messages to solve. I'm pretty good at figuring them out." I twisted my swing toward

Nicholas. "Do you remember what Mr. Schneider's message sounded like?"

"It was too complicated to memorize," he said. "What we need to do is record it on tape. That way, we can listen to it over and over until we solve it. That's how they do it in the spy shows my dad watches."

I sighed. "So Mr. Schneider has to come back?"

"He has to come anyway for your lesson, doesn't he?" Frank asked.

I nodded, trying not to think about those razor-sharp fangs.

"Of course, that's not until Friday," Nicholas said. He tapped the swing's metal chain with his fingers. "Is there any way you can get him to come over sooner?"

I didn't really want him to come over sooner—or at all. But I knew I needed to try.

"I guess I can ask my mom."

Nicholas nodded. "Good. And when he shows up, we'll be ready."

CHAPTER 19
BEGGING FOR A BRUISING

Mom sat in the living room reading her magazine while I practiced piano. Was I sending a message to the white van Bermuda Triangle alien spacecraft? Outside, the sky had turned dark, but there were no signs I'd made contact. I wished Frank had left his telescope in my backyard so I could see if the UFO was hovering above my house. Maybe that was the answer. Maybe Frank and Nicholas needed to hang out in the backyard and keep an eye up above while Mr. Schneider played piano.

"I think I need another lesson," I said to Mom while still peering out the window. I couldn't believe the words were coming out of my mouth, but I had to think of the big picture. There was a lot at stake: finding the boy from Mayson, capturing the white van werewolf alien kidnappers, solving the mystery of the Bermuda Triangle, and a $3,000 reward. "Yes," I added firmly. "I definitely need another lesson."

"You need a lot more than one." Alice walked into the room with the same scowl she'd had on her face since Mom and Dad had grounded her.

Mom raised her head from her magazine and gave Alice her *knock it off* look.

"All I'm saying," Alice continued, "is that he's no Beethoven."

"No one's making you stay here and listen," I told her.

"Where am I supposed to go? I can hear you in my room. I can hear you in *every* room. And it's not like I'm allowed to leave this prison." She threw herself on the chair opposite Mom and crossed her arms over her chest.

"Enough with the dramatics," Mom said. "You're doing just fine, Danny. You'll get there. Even Beethoven wasn't Beethoven right away."

"Who was he, then?" I asked.

She laughed. "Well, he was Beethoven, of course. What I meant was that I'm sure it took many years of hard work before he became a master at his craft."

"Exactly," I said. "That's why I need another lesson."

"Mr. Schneider's coming on Friday like he always does. Until then, keep practicing." Mom went back to her magazine.

"What I mean is that I need another lesson before Friday."

She closed the magazine. "But you just had one yesterday. Three in one week would be a little much, even for Beethoven."

"I know," I said. "But I really feel like I'm close to a breakthrough." It wasn't actually a lie; it just had nothing to do with my piano-playing skills. Plus, I was pretty sure that when you were lying for the sake of saving the universe, you got a pass. "I'm afraid that if I wait until Friday, I might lose . . . *it*."

Mom scrunched her face in a way that made her appear like she had almost as many wrinkles as Mrs. Albertini. Maybe that's how Mrs. Albertini got so many wrinkles. Maybe she scrunched her face too many times. Before I could warn Mom, her face went back to normal. "And what is *it*?" she asked.

"You know," I said. Of course, *it* meant the

chance to catch Mr. Schneider and the aliens before they struck again, but I couldn't say that to Mom. I slowly swung my arm across the front of the piano, displaying it like it was a prize on one of those game shows she liked to watch, and said, "This." I smiled and hoped my weird demonstration was enough to convince her.

"You're even more of a dork than I thought," my sister said.

Mom put the magazine back on the coffee table. "Alice, I'm assuming you don't want to add another week to your punishment."

My sister glared at me. It figured that she blamed me for Mom's reprimand. Even if I proved Mr. Schneider was the white van kidnapper, even if I showed that aliens were real, even if I helped find the missing boy, Alice would still blame me for something.

Mom tilted her head while she talked to me. "What is this really about, Danny? I usually have to beg you to play the piano. Does this have something to do with a girl? Is that it?"

"What? No! I just . . . I'm starting to like playing, okay? And I want an extra lesson. I have some allowance saved up, if that helps."

"No, it's okay," Mom said. "Whatever the reason, I'm just glad you're finally showing an interest. I suppose I could call Mr. Schneider to see if he's available tomorrow. And you can save your money, although that's very sweet. We have a little extra now with your father's promotion."

"Thanks," I told her. "When's Dad getting home anyway?" It was almost eight o'clock. For as long as I could remember, Dad had always worked the same steady day schedule. The only time Dad ever worked this late was a couple of years ago when half the factory was home sick with the flu.

"He should be home any minute," Mom said. "Mr. Santone changed his schedule. Every day is different now. He doesn't know if he's coming or going. The poor man's a mess. So you two need to be on your best behavior, okay? He's already on edge as it is without your bickering adding to it."

"Why'd they change his hours?" I asked.

"They're probably just trying something new," Mom said with a half-smile. "They do that every once in a while."

I half-smiled back even though I didn't remember that ever happening before.

"I heard you went back to visit Mrs. Albertini

yesterday after school," Mom continued. "Her son Anthony told me when I stopped in at the market earlier. Did she need help with something?"

"No," I told her. "I just felt like visiting."

Alice fake-coughed to cover the sound of her saying, "Weirdo." Mom gave her another warning look.

"Well, that's lovely," Mom said. "I'm sure she appreciated the company."

"She's so old. What do you even talk about?" Alice asked.

"I don't know," I told her. "Just stuff. She was telling me about Oxly. That's where she's from."

"Wow. *Neat.*" Alice rolled her eyes. "Oh, speaking of Oxly. I heard there was another attempted white van kidnapping. Yesterday. Ray Lanzo was talking about it in the cafeteria today."

"What?" Mom sounded worried. "I didn't hear about that. What happened? Do they think it was the same person? Did anyone see anything?" Mom's voice grew more frantic with each question.

"Frank said the girl ran away before anything could happen," I told her.

"That's not what Ray said," Alice told us. "He saw everything."

"He was there? What did he see? Did he tell the police?" Mom asked.

"Well . . ." Alice began. She glanced at me and smirked. "I don't know who he told, but he said the little girl was walking down the street when the white van pulled up next to her. When she screamed, there was a flash in the sky, and a fire-breathing dragon swooshed down out of the clouds. The van drove away before the dragon's breath could fully reach it, but Ray's pretty sure there might be some burn marks on the back. Then the little girl did this whirly-twirly thing and transformed into a super-hero with a cape and mask and everything. She and the dragon flew away in her magic spaceship." Alice laughed so hard she snorted.

"Really, Alice," Mom said. "It's not funny. A missing child is nothing to make light of."

I had to agree, although I also wondered if I should jot down the part about possible burn marks on the back of the van in my Super-Secret Spy Note-book. Probably not. I'd already written my ninth entry as soon as I got home from school:

9. *Mr. Schneider is using my piano to send messages to the UFO.*

The front door flew open before any of us could say anything else about Oxly, the girl, the white van, dragons, or magic spaceships.

"Howard!" Mom jumped up and cried, "What happened?"

Dad walked into the living room, his left eye bruised and swollen shut.

CHAPTER 20
PURPLE SOUP

Dad insisted he'd walked into a wall, but I knew that wasn't true. I could tell Alice didn't believe him either because she kept asking questions like "How could a wall just hit only your eye and no other part of your face?" and, "If you walked into something flat, why is the bruise so round?"

Finally, Dad sat up on the sofa and took the frozen bag of peas he'd been using as an icepack off his face. "I told you already," he snapped. "That's what happened. Now leave me alone. I've got a pounding headache." He put the bag back over his eye, and Mom ushered Alice and me out of the living room.

After school the next day, I stopped at Mrs. Albertini's house.

As usual, two plates were already out when I walked into her kitchen. A loaf of Scholly's chocolate-frosted pound cake sat in the middle of the table. I waited for Mrs. Albertini to cut two slices for us, but instead, she kept stirring a pot that was on the stove.

"First, borscht," she said. "Then cake." She ladled some soup into a bowl. "I thought you might like to try some after our talk the other day." A sly smile crossed her face. "My mother somehow convinced that couple in Larston to give up their recipe. Then she taught me how to make it. I had to swear never to speak a word of it to my bubbe. In fact, I've really never spoke about it to anyone. Look at me, telling you all of my secrets." She placed the steamy bowl in front of me. "Go ahead, try it."

"It's purple," I noted. It was also lumpy with weird vegetables floating around, and it smelled like stinky feet. I kept that to myself since Mrs. Albertini seemed so excited about her gloppy soup.

"It gets its color from the beets," she explained.

If she was trying to convince me to eat this slop, saying it was made from beets wasn't the way to do it. Once, Mom tried to fool me into eating beets by telling me they were grape Jell-O. The minute I took the first bite, I choked so badly on the disgusting taste that I nearly hurled right there at the dinner table. Mom never tried to make me eat them again.

Mrs. Albertini dropped a blob of white goop into my bowl. "I forgot the sour cream," she said. "Adds a little extra flavor."

With my spoon, I made white circular swirls through the purple. That's what I did when I didn't want to eat something. I swirled.

Mrs. Albertini laughed. "You're having the same reaction my Anthony had the first time I served him borscht. I suppose it's an acquired taste. That's all right—maybe you'll feel like trying it another time." She whisked away the bowl and placed a hearty piece of cake on my plate instead. "I think you'll like this better."

"Thanks," I told her. And then, since I felt bad that I didn't want to try her secret recipe, I added, "The color was kind of cool. I never saw purple soup before."

She sat back down and swallowed three big spoonfuls from the bowl of soup, one after another. "Ahh," she said. "You don't know what you're missing." She wiped her mouth with her napkin and smiled. "So what brings you by today? Is your friend still giving you a hard time?"

"No," I told her. "Some of the other kids are, but he's not. We're friends again. Did Anthony have trouble with the kids at school? When he was my age?"

She brought her bowl over to the sink and filled her kettle for tea. That's how I knew it was a hard question. Mrs. Albertini always seemed to make tea when I asked her tough questions. She sat back down, but her smile had disappeared.

"It wasn't easy growing up Jewish in Oxly. My father used to say he was glad I was a girl—that the kids would have done worse than shout awful words if I were a boy. But the words were bad enough. I didn't want Anthony to go through what I went through."

"So no one knew he was Jewish?"

"Some knew, I suppose," she said. "Those who remembered Lillian Gerstein. But they also knew he had another side that wasn't Jewish. People see what they want to see. We never lied to anyone. We just kept it more to ourselves, to make things easier. The same way your parents seem to keep it to themselves."

"But it hasn't been easier for us."

She nodded. "I'm sorry. I know how hard it is. I don't know if I will ever understand the hatred some people have. But it's not everybody, and knowing there are good people in this town is what keeps me here. It's what keeps your parents here too. Just look at your friend. I had a feeling he'd be back. I'm so glad to hear the two of you have made up." She got up to pour her tea.

I nodded. "We hung out in my backyard the other day. Just like you and your friends used to do."

"How lovely. When Marge, Sally, and I used to get together, we'd stare up at the clouds and search for things."

"What kinds of things?" I asked.

"Hearts and bunnies and silly shapes like that. They were the clouds, of course, but when we stared at them long enough, they almost came alive."

"We search for UFOs and aliens. Real ones." I knew I wasn't supposed to tell anyone, but since Mrs. Albertini trusted me with her secrets, I figured I owed her at least one secret of my own.

"My! That's exciting," Mrs. Albertini said. "Have you seen any?"

"Nicholas did, but it was going too fast, and I missed it. We were pretty sure it was the one that belonged to—" I stopped myself before mentioning Mr. Schneider.

"Belonged to?" Mrs. Albertini asked.

"Oh," I stumbled. "Well, my friend Frank read an article about some scientist who thinks the missing planes and boats in the Bermuda Triangle were actually stolen by aliens. I don't know. It's just a dumb theory."

"I think it sounds perfectly reasonable," Mrs. Albertini said. She put another slice of cake on my plate. "Here—you need to keep up your strength if you're going to solve one of the world's greatest mysteries."

"Thanks," I said. "Can I ask you something else?"

"You can ask me as many things as you like."

"I told you my dad got that promotion, right?"

"It's wonderful news," she replied.

"Well, it would be, except his whole schedule is messed up now. He works a different shift every day. Mom says the factory bosses change things up every now and again, but I don't ever remember that happening before. And he barely gets to sleep. Do you remember that happening with Mr. Albertini?"

"I don't recall, but they may run things differently now. Who's to say? Anyway, with the excitement of his promotion, he probably won't even notice the inconvenience."

"That's not the only inconvenience," I muttered.

"What?" she asked.

"At the factory. He got a black eye." I watched as the wrinkles on Mrs. Albertini's face fell into a frown, then added, "He said he walked into a wall. But I know that's not what really happened."

Mrs. Albertini looked away and sighed. Then she took another sip of her tea.

CHAPTER 21
CRACKING THE CODE

I raced through our front door and shoved a plastic container into Mom's hands. "I'm here! I didn't forget!" Collapsing into the chair by the entry table, I tried to catch my breath. Mrs. Albertini lived close to us, but I'd still sprinted the entire way home. "Wait," I said. "Why are you home? It's Wednesday!"

"I switched with one of the other nurses," Mom replied. "I'm working late tomorrow. What is this?" She lifted the covered plastic bowl up to the light to examine its contents.

"Borsht." I stood back up now that I could breathe again. "It's purple soup. Made from beets."

"I know what borscht is," she replied. "Where'd it come from?"

"Mrs. Albertini," I told her. "Some secret recipe.

She gave it to me on my way home."

"So very thoughtful," Mom said. "I'll give her a call to thank her after dinner."

"Is Mr. Schneider here yet?" Mom and I were the only ones in the living room, but that didn't mean he wasn't about to slither out from some corner or doorway. You just never knew with aliens.

"No," Mom said, "and it's a good thing. I went to a lot of trouble getting this extra lesson for you today. He wouldn't appreciate you being late." She walked into the kitchen and put the soup on the counter. "Your father loves borscht. I'll heat this up for him when he gets home later. It's just what he needs to cheer him up."

"You mean 'cause of his wall injury?"

Mom turned away. It was the same thing Mrs. Albertini had done when I'd told her about it. I could tell Mrs. Albertini had been upset by the news, but she'd already made her tea. So instead, she got up and packed some borscht for Mom. That's when I noticed the time and remembered Mr. Schneider was coming over. So I ran home as fast as I could with the container of secret purple soup.

I walked to the back door, stretching my neck to look around the yard through the window.

"What are you doing?" Mom asked. "You're acting strange."

"Huh?" I replied. "Oh. I thought I heard something."

Nicholas and Frank had promised to sneak into the backyard during my music lesson, but I didn't see them yet. The plan was for them to bring Frank's telescope and watch for UFOs while Mr. Schneider played. After my lesson, we'd try to crack the code and figure out the message from the tape recording.

The tape recording! I'd forgotten all about setting up my portable tape recorder next to the piano.

"I'll be right back." I ran upstairs to find my equipment.

"But, Daniel!" Mom called. "Mr. Schneider will be here any second!"

She was right. As soon as I grabbed the tape recorder from my bedroom, the doorbell rang. I shoved it behind my back and headed down the steps.

My werewolf alien piano teacher walked into the living room. "Hello, Mrs. Wexler; Daniel." His voice sounded extra creepy.

"Mr. Schneider, thank you so much for squeezing us in again," said Mom.

"As it turned out," he said, "I had a cancellation." He tapped his hairy fingers together as he spoke, and I wished I'd already started recording. His tapping had to mean something important. I hoped Nicholas and Frank were out back by now.

"Perfect," Mom said. She placed the envelope with his money on the entry table and grabbed her jacket.

"You're leaving?" I asked. How could she leave me all alone with an alien kidnapper? Was she out of her mind?

"Yes, Danny. I just have to run to the market for a few things. I won't be long."

"Right. Okay." At least Alice was upstairs—not that she'd protect me or anything.

Mom walked out the door. I smiled at Mr. Schneider, but he didn't smile back, which was actually a good thing since I didn't want to see his fangs again.

He placed his coat across the chair by the front window and took his usual seat at the piano before opening his briefcase to pull out his music.

"A tape recorder?" he asked.

Shoot. I'd tried to place it on the bench next to me where I thought he might not see it. "Oh, I um—"

"Did you want to record our lesson?"

"I, uh, well—" I thought of running for the front door, but I'd seen the way Mr. Schneider scurried away at the end of our lessons. He was fast. And who knew what powers were in those hairy fingers. I wondered if they were weapons. Like, finger number one probably shot out some kind of instant freezing power, while finger number two maybe turned things into balls of fire. And the others could probably do awful things too, like maybe zap kids directly to the spaceship even without the white van. Especially when he was mad about catching someone recording his alien messages.

I shut my eyes and braced myself, hoping my doomed fate wouldn't be too painful.

"Yes," Mr. Schneider said, "I think you should record our lesson. It's an excellent idea, actually. It will help with your practices. Good thinking."

"What?" I asked, opening my eyes. "I mean, yeah, okay."

With shaky fingers, I pressed the red and black buttons to start the device, making sure the spindles inside the tape were turning. Mr. Schneider started moving his skinny, hair-covered fingers across the piano keys.

The lesson actually went fine, which was weird, because lessons with Mr. Schneider were never fine. There was always *something*.

Mom walked back in with her groceries just as Mr. Schneider was putting his coat on to leave. "How did everything go?" she nervously asked. Even Mom knew my lessons never went well.

"I've noticed improvement," Mr. Schneider said. "I'll see you Friday, Daniel?"

I nodded. Mr. Schneider said goodbye to Mom, grabbed his envelope, and rushed off.

"Danny," Mom said, hanging her jacket up, "Nicholas and Frank are in our backyard. Are you expecting them?"

Right! I'd almost forgotten the rest of our plan. "Yes—I mean, maybe? I have to get something first. Thanks."

I grabbed my tape recorder, ran upstairs to collect my Super-Secret Spy Notebook, and headed out the back door.

"Did you get it?" Nicholas asked.

"Yeah." I pointed to the tape recorder. "What about out here?"

"Didn't see anything," Frank said. "Not even a plane or a bird."

I pressed the Rewind button on the machine, and the three of us sat on the edge of the patio listening to the whirling of the tape going back to its starting point.

The machine stopped.

"Ready?" I asked. I pressed Play before either of them answered. The recording started with Mr. Schneider playing piano, then him teaching me the very end of the song from where we left off last time. After that, I had my turn to try the song. Alice was right: I was horrible. Maybe extra lessons weren't such a bad idea. Since we knew *I* wasn't a werewolf Bermuda Triangle alien sending secret messages, I fast-forwarded through those parts. Why torture my friends? After a few more rounds of him showing me stuff and me playing it, Mr. Schneider announced that my time was up. That was it. Pretty boring, especially since it was the second time I was sitting through it.

"Did you hear anything?" I asked.

"Sounded like that Beethoven song," Frank said.

"It *was* that Beethoven song. I meant something other than that."

Nicholas grabbed the recorder from my lap and pushed the Rewind and Forward buttons a few times to find a particular spot in the tape. "Here," he said. "Right here. It's while he's talking to you, and it's not loud, but he's definitely hitting some keys that aren't part of the song. Just like last time."

We all leaned in and listened closely.

"I hear it now," Frank said. "But what does it mean?"

I listened to it a few more times and thought about everything my spy book had taught me about cracking codes. Rule number one was to pull out the pattern, but there was no pattern to it at all. Then it hit me. I grabbed the recorder away from Nicholas. "Stop!" I yelled. "Don't play it anymore."

"Why?" he asked. "Wasn't that the whole point of recording it?"

"It's a trick," I said. "Mr. Schneider knew I was taping. He even said it was a good idea."

"So?" Frank asked.

I opened my Super-Secret Spy Notebook.

10. Mr. Schneider knows.

"Mr. Schneider knows what?" Frank asked.

"About this," I explained. "Mr. Schneider never agrees with me or thinks any of my ideas are any good. And you didn't see anything while I was in my lesson, right? Maybe Mr. Schneider knew that the UFO wasn't going to be around tonight, so he had me record his message knowing I'd play it again later in the week to help me practice. He's using us to call the UFO. He's using us to help kidnap kids."

"You're right!" Nicholas said. "So now what do we do?"

I grinned. "Mr. Schneider doesn't know *we* know. All we have to do is beat him at his own game. And that means we keep playing the tape. And we keep watching every night until the UFO hears it and comes back."

"Then we turn over the tape and Mr. Schneider before he can actually kidnap anyone else," said Frank. "And we collect our reward."

CHAPTER 22
LIBRARY RULES

We had two days to go before spring break officially started. No one was in the mood to be in school, including Mrs. Greely. She didn't even say *settle down* after the morning bell rang, and we definitely needed to settle down. Frank, Nicholas, and I huddled around Frank's desk talking about everything we wanted to do over our week off. Our big plans included proving Mr. Schneider was an alien kidnapper, finding the boy from Mayson, solving the Bermuda Triangle mystery, and collecting our reward. Also, there was a rumor that *Star Wars* might be coming back to the Picture Palace, and this time, we'd be sure to get there super early. Even alien hunters needed a break now and again.

After a few minutes, Mrs. Greely announced,

"I've arranged some extra library time this morning so you can all work on your presidents project before break."

Eugene Barone raised his hand.

"Yes, Eugene?" Mrs. Greely asked.

"But it's Thursday. We always have science and math in the mornings on Thursdays."

Joey Simone fake-coughed *"Nerd"* and the entire class laughed, including me. Yeah, I knew it was wrong. And I started to feel bad. I cleared my throat and brushed pretend lint off my sleeve while everyone else continued.

"I thought going to the library would be a better use of our time," said Mrs. Greely. "We can pick up math and science after the break."

"What about tomorrow?" Eugene asked, this time without raising his hand.

"It's a half day. I had planned on showing a movie, but only if you're all well behaved today. Let's try to do better, shall we?"

Maria Martona was next to raise her hand.

Mrs. Greely looked exhausted, and it wasn't even 9:30 in the morning. "No, Maria," she said, without even letting her ask her question. "You can't work in pairs when you get to the library. You may sit together at tables, but as I've told you several times already, this is an independent project."

"This is so great," Nicholas whispered as we headed down the hallway toward the library. "Mrs. Greely might as well have given us indoor recess all morning. It's pretty much the same thing."

"It's better," Frank said. "Mrs. Greely hardly ever sticks around during library time. That's probably why she gave it to us, so she could go hang out in the teacher's lounge while we're there."

"You know the plan, right?" Nicholas asked.

I nodded.

The plan was to get *the table*. The one buried deep in the back corner behind the shelf with the boring poetry books that nobody ever wanted to read. It was also the table that was as far away from Mrs. Milo's desk as possible. She was the school librarian and was a thousand years old. Her glasses reminded me of the magnifying glass Dad bought me to go with my spy book. They were that thick, and they made her eyes huge too. She also always shouted when she spoke, which I thought was funny since she worked in the library where everyone was supposed to be quiet. Mom said it was because she had trouble hearing. I didn't believe that, though, 'cause even if we were all the way in the back of the room and trying to keep our voices low, she yelled at us to keep it down. Still, the farther away you were from her, the better.

As soon as we got to the library, the three of us raced to the back of the room. Frank threw his notebook on the table, but he threw it so fast that it slid right off. When he bent down to pick it up, Bobby pulled out a chair and sat down.

"Hey, I was here first," Frank said, standing back up.

"No, I was," Bobby insisted.

Joey and Vincent sat down at the table with him.

"That's not true," I said. I knew it wasn't going to end well as soon as I opened my mouth. But it was too late. I was mad—and not just about the table. "Frank put his notebook down first. It just fell off, that's all. This is *our* table." I hoped Mrs. Greely or Mrs. Milo would step in, but I didn't see either of them in the room.

Joey stood up and scowled at Frank. "So you've got Matzah Boy doing your dirty work? Makes perfect sense, since he's dirty just like his father."

"You take that back!" I yelled, getting right up into his face. I stood on my tiptoes and everything.

"Danny, come on." Nicholas pulled on my sleeve. "He's not worth it."

"No," I said, not budging. "He needs to take it back."

"*You* need to step away," Joey said, staring me down.

Frank pulled at my other sleeve so hard I stumbled backward. "Let's go," he said to Nicholas and me. "We didn't want to sit here anyway."

"He shouldn't have said that." My heart raced, thumping so loudly that I could barely hear my own words. I began to walk away but turned around once more to see Joey spit on the spot where I'd been standing. Then he traced an imaginary cross on his body with his hands: forehead to chest, then shoulder to shoulder.

We sat at a table as far away from them as possible. It wasn't our original plan, but in my mind, it was an even better plan.

"Why did he do that?" I asked. "Why did Joey spit and make that cross?"

"You don't want to know," Frank said.

"I asked the question, didn't I?"

Frank glanced at Nicholas, then back at me. "My grandma—Nonna—she does that whenever she thinks something or someone is cursed."

"So they think I'm cursed?" I asked.

"They think a lot of stupid things," Nicholas said.

"Here's what I think," I told them, my anger building up. "I think I'm going to start telling Mr. Schneider about Joey, Bobby, and Vincent. Talk them up, you know? Maybe he'll zap them into his white van alien spacecraft. They're the ones who should go live on Mars, not some innocent little kid from Mayson." I stopped, partly 'cause it sounded ridiculous and partly 'cause it actually wasn't a half-bad idea. Then I started laughing. I started laughing so hard I couldn't stop, even though I knew it was mean. Frank and Nicholas started laughing too.

"Boys!" Mrs. Milo walked into the room and cracked her ruler across her desk. Oh, sure, now she was around.

"Sorry," I said, clamping my hand over my mouth. I lowered my voice back down to my quietest whisper. "You're coming over later, right? To my backyard? I feel like something big is gonna happen tonight."

"Yeah, I'll be there," Frank said. "Hey, do you think I can just leave my telescope this time? It's kind of heavy to lug back and forth. My parents won't care. As long as we bring it inside when we're done."

"It's fine with me," I said. "What about you?" I asked Nicholas.

"I don't know," he said hesitantly.

"You don't know if Frank should leave his telescope, or you don't know if you're coming over?"

"The second part," he said. "I want to, but my mom was asking a lot of questions when I got home yesterday about where I'd been. It made me real nervous."

"Do you think she knows?" I asked.

He shrugged. "Maybe."

Mrs. Milo cracked her ruler again even though we were barely making any noise. We opened our notebooks and pretended to write.

"Don't worry," Nicholas whispered. "I'll figure something out." He shook his head and said, "It's not right."

I agreed, but it didn't make me feel any better.

CHAPTER 23
MAKING CONTACT

In the morning, Mom reminded us she'd be working late because she'd switched shifts at the hospital. It wasn't a big deal, except now that Dad's schedule was all weird, he'd be working late tonight too. Mom told Alice and me that we should just heat up a couple of frozen TV dinners for ourselves. I didn't mind. Some of them were okay, like the one that had fried chicken, corn, and chocolate pudding. And even if I got stuck with the one that had the nasty peas or green beans, there wouldn't be any adults around, so I'd be able to skip the vegetable part and go right to the dessert. Alice hated them, though—even the ones that weren't half bad. When I told Mom it would be fine, Alice rolled her eyes at me.

That made me think about how she complained that I never helped enough with dinner. And then I got the brilliant idea to make Mrs. Albertini's rolled cabbage. Why not? It seemed easy enough, and it made a lot, so there'd be enough left for Mom and Dad when they got home later. They probably wouldn't want frozen TV dinners either. Plus, Frank was coming to my house this afternoon, and he was a pretty decent cook. Once, he made English muffin pizzas in the toaster oven, and they tasted really good.

On the way home from school, I stopped at Mrs. Albertini's house to ask her for the rolled cabbage recipe. She wrote it down with step-by-step instructions, and then she called Anthony at the market and gave him the list of ingredients I would need. By the time I got to the market, everything was packed up and waiting for me. It had also been paid for, which was good, 'cause I hadn't actually thought about that part. Frank met me at my house.

"I thought you said this was easy," he said as he struggled to roll up his cabbage. It tore in half, and all the meat fell out into the soupy tomato sauce in the baking pan. He threw the torn cabbage on top of it and started with a new piece.

"You overstuffed. You can't overstuff," I said, remembering Mrs. Albertini's advice. Except my cabbage did the exact same thing. I shrugged and threw my unrolled roll into the pan with his.

"What's going on in here?" Alice's scowl was nastier than usual.

"We're cooking dinner tonight," I said.

"Why?" she asked, crossing her arms. "What are you two up to?"

"Nothing," I told her. "We're trying to be helpful. You're always complaining I don't help. And you said you didn't want a TV dinner."

"What is it?" She peered into the pan with that face she always made when something smelled disgusting.

"Rolled cabbage." I held up the instruction sheet from Mrs. Albertini.

She snorted and filled a large pot with water.

"What are you doing?" I asked.

"Making spaghetti. I wasn't planning on eating one of those foul TV dinners. It's bad enough I have to stay inside this prison; I don't need food poisoning too. Is that what you're trying to do? Is this revenge for Terri and me scaring you?"

"No. I already told you. We're just trying to help. Whatever. Just forget it."

"Done." She grabbed the box of pasta from the cabinet. "You want some, Frank, or are you eating that?"

He glanced at our pan. We didn't have a single rolled roll. Just lumps of meat, onions, and rice floating in watery red soup with large pieces of cabbage scattered in between. It looked worse than Mrs. Albertini's gloppy purple borscht, but maybe it would magically morph together in the oven.

"Nah, I'm good," he said.

A knock at the door startled me. Frank jumped too.

"Who's that?" I half-whispered.

"Hopefully a pizza delivery," Alice said, walking into the living room.

I wasn't laughing. What if the aliens had gotten Mr. Schneider's message last night? What if they knew about our plan and were here to grab the tape before we could turn it over to the police? Or worse, what if they were here to grab *us*? Alice headed toward the door to let in the clan of hairy-handed werewolf aliens.

"No!" I yelled as she reached out to turn the knob. "We're not supposed to answer the door when Mom and Dad aren't here."

"It's just Nicholas," she said, swinging it open. "Jeez, you're such a doofus."

Nicholas stepped inside. He raised his eyebrows at Alice and gave her some weird smile.

"I hate my life," she mumbled and marched back into the kitchen.

Nicholas watched her the whole way. "She said my name," he murmured in amazement.

"She said my name earlier," Frank said. "You don't see me getting all goofy."

"What are you doing here?" I asked. "What'd you tell your mom?"

"Told her I was going out to do some research." Nicholas pointed to his book bag.

"And she just let you go?" I asked.

"I think she thought I meant schoolwork at the library. You know, for the president project. She's not going to say no to that."

"What if she checks up on you?" Frank asked.

"I'll say I was at your house. I never said I was going to the library. You'll cover for me, right?"

"Sure," Frank said.

"Anyway, I don't have a lot of time," he added.

I ran upstairs to get the Super-Secret Spy Notebook and the tape recorder. Then we put the pan of soupy unrolled cabbage in the oven and headed outside. I pulled over the chairs from the patio while Frank set up the telescope. Nicholas found the exact spot in the recording where Mr. Schneider played his secret message. He played it three times while Frank kept watch through the telescope.

"Nothing," Frank said.

Nicholas and I kept watch too in case we spotted something for Frank to zoom in on.

"How many times do you think we should play it?" I asked.

"At least ten," Nicholas responded. He hit the Rewind and Play buttons again. The sky darkened, and thick clouds moved in.

"Still nothing," Frank said.

Nicholas hit Rewind and Play again. As Mr. Schneider played the final piano key on the message we all knew by heart after hearing it so many times, the wind picked up. The tiny hairs on my arms started to prickle and rise. All around us, the leaves on the trees and bushes rustled. I nervously glanced at Nicholas. Frank kept a steady watch through his telescope, his hair blowing around in the wind. Then, without warning, a flash of light filled the sky. Nicholas and I jumped out of our seats.

"Run!" Frank yelled. He grabbed his telescope, and we all sprinted back into the house, slamming the door tight behind us. "I saw it!" he cried as we raced into the living room, as far away from the backyard as possible. "A bolt! Aimed right at us. They were trying to snatch us!"

"Scared of a little thunderstorm?" Alice laughed. She was sitting on the couch, eating her bowl of spaghetti.

"That's no thunderstorm," I told her, clutching my Super-Secret Spy Notebook.

"Sure it is." Alice pointed to the television screen. A reporter wearing a brown suit stood in front of a weather map, pointing to clouds and bolts of lightning. "Coming from Oxly. Said the rain is going to start any minute." She pointed toward the ceiling as the sound of pouring rain hitting the roof began. A rumble of thunder followed. "And there it is." To Frank and Nicholas, she said, "Sure you don't want some spaghetti? You might be stuck here awhile."

Panic crossed Nicholas's face, and I couldn't tell if it had to do more with the failed alien abduction or the possibility of his mom catching him at my house.

"No, thanks," Frank said, his voice still shaky. "I'll call my mom to pick us up," he told Nicholas. "It'll be fine."

Then we waited in the living room and barely spoke. After Frank and Nicholas left, I paced around the whole house, thinking about what had happened, while the storm continued to rage outside.

Mom got home just before I went to bed. She even ate some of my unrolled cabbage, which didn't come out completely terrible. But between worrying if Nicholas made it home without getting in trouble and wondering if the storm was actually the aliens swooping in with their UFO to make a move, I couldn't fall asleep at all. Then I thought of something. I opened my Super-Secret Spy Notebook.

11. The movie!

Now I was more awake than ever. When I heard Dad get home an hour later, I decided to go say hello to him and maybe make some warm milk to help me get back to bed, but three steps down the stairs, I stopped.

"She had no business sticking her nose in where it didn't belong," Dad snapped.

I peeked through the banister long enough to see that he was holding another bag of frozen vegetables up to his face. This time, it covered his cheek.

"Shh," Mom said, "The kids will hear. Lola didn't intend any harm. She was just trying to help."

"I wouldn't be in this mess if it wasn't for her *help*." Dad lowered his voice, "I don't need old Lola Albertini butting in. I can get my own promotion, and I can fight my own fight."

CHAPTER 24
THE MURDERIST

I didn't sleep well the rest of the night. I kept thinking about the alien thunderstorm, hoping Nicholas didn't get in trouble for sneaking over to my house, and hearing Dad's words about Mrs. Albertini.

In the morning, Nicholas's bus pulled up to the school just as Frank and I arrived.

"Well?" I asked. "Did you get in trouble yesterday?"

"Nah," he said. "My mom saw me get out of Frank's mom's car and didn't ask any questions. I guess she figured we were both at the library. She only said she was glad I was home and out of the storm."

"My mom said the same thing," Frank noted. "And our lights kept going on and off. I didn't sleep at all last night."

"Me, neither," I said. "The whole thing was awfully creepy."

"So we all agree that it was . . ." Frank looked around and then mouthed, "the UFO."

"It had to be," Nicholas said. "Every time we played that recording, it got darker and windier. Right up until the last time." He leaned in real close to Frank and me and, "*BAM!*" He clapped his hands together, making me flinch. "Mr. Schneider's message got through, that's for sure."

"What do you think about the rain?" I asked.

"It had to be a cover by the aliens," Nicholas said. "Nothing suspicious about a rainstorm, right?"

"But how did they do it?" Frank asked. "The rain part, I mean?"

He shrugged. "How would I know? Do I look like an alien? They can just do stuff. That's all."

It seemed like a reasonable answer.

"Hey, Frank," I said. "Remember when we saw that Bermuda Triangle movie?"

"Sure," he said. "What about it?"

"Well, right before we left, there was a huge rumble of thunder—like a storm was coming—and that *something bad is about to happen* music was playing."

Frank's eyes widened. "Right! That's how the

aliens captured the stuff in the Bermuda Triangle. They made a storm and then zapped up boats and planes using lightning so it didn't look suspicious. Danny, you've totally figured it out."

"Wow. It's kind of genius," Nicholas said.

I nodded. "Now what do we do?"

At that moment, the first bell rang. Once we passed through the front doors of the school, all talk of piano-playing, white-van-driving, Bermuda Triangle werewolf aliens was supposed to be on hold, but no one had answered my question about what to do next. I was just about to bring it up again when my body slammed into the wall next to me.

"Ow!" I yelled. Pain seared up my arm.

"Watch it, freak," Joey Simone sneered.

"Why don't you watch it?" Frank said.

I rubbed my shoulder. There was no sign of Vincent or Bobby. Joey was alone on this one.

"I'm always watching," Joey said. He stood so close to Frank that I was sure Frank could see right up his nose. Then he turned and walked down the hallway.

"Jerk," Nicholas said. For a second I thought Joey heard 'cause he seemed to slow down, but then he disappeared through the classroom doorway. Nicholas turned to me. "You okay?"

I nodded and adjusted my book bag.

The day went pretty smoothly until art class. Mr. Lane gave us each a large lump of clay and did a brief demonstration on how to use the carving tools to create a head with a face and hair. Then he told us to give it a try. He said we should be creative, and he never specified that we had to make a *human* head, so I turned mine into a werewolf alien with a super-hairy face, fangs for teeth, and a bald head. I took a step back and admired my work. I'd never seen Mr. Schneider as a full-on werewolf, but I was pretty sure I'd come close to the real deal with my clay head.

"Okay, class." Mr. Lane clapped his hands together to get our attention. "Finish up and put your initials on the bottom. I'll fire these up in the kiln over spring break, and we'll paint and glaze them when you return."

I was just about to show Frank and Nicholas my work when Joey walked by. He stared me square in the eyes before swiping my head right off the table. My clay head, not my real head. It fell to the ground with a thud.

"Oops," he said, his eyes staying on mine the entire time.

I picked up my project. My werewolf alien face was completely flattened, and there was a gash near the top of the head.

"Hey!" I yelled. "You ruined my project!"

"I think it's much better now," Joey said. "You shouldn't keep your stuff so close to the edge where people can knock into it when they're just walking by."

Mr. Lane sent Joey to the principal's office. Then he took the clay head, smoothed out the gash, and fixed up the face. "There," he said. "Good as new."

"Thanks," I told him. It did look good as new, but it didn't look like my werewolf alien anymore.

I carved my initials on the bottom and walked it over to the shelf with the other finished projects.

Joey returned from the principal's office five minutes after we got back to Mrs. Greely's room. He glared at me while he walked to his seat. Mrs. Greely rolled a cart carrying a movie projector to the center of the room and pulled down the big white screen in front of the chalkboard. She'd decided to show us a movie. I was hoping for something cool like *Escape to Witch Mountain*, but it was *Willy Wonka and the Chocolate Factory*. I guess that was okay, but I'd already seen it a bunch of times.

Halfway through the movie, a folded-up note landed on my desk. I figured it was from Frank, but when I glanced over to him, he was fast asleep. Had Nicholas turned around and tossed it over? I checked to see if Mrs. Greely was watching, but she was busy reading a magazine. I carefully opened the note.

You're next.

From two rows over, Joey stared right at me and punched his fist into his palm. *You're next?* What did that mean? Next after who?

I pictured my clay head smashed on the ground, all flattened with that giant gash. It reminded me of Dad with his bruised eye and injured cheek. A cold sweat formed across the tingling hairs on my neck. I slid out of my seat and walked to the front of the class.

"Yes, Daniel?" Mrs. Greely asked. "Are you okay?"

"I don't feel so great," I told her.

She handed me the nurse pass.

Nurse Stanton put a cold cloth on my forehead, took my temperature, and let me rest on one of the cots by the window.

"The day is just about over," she said after some time had gone by. "Go ahead back to your class-room. You seem fine now."

I walked slowly. Really slowly. The movie was

just finishing as I took my seat. Mrs. Greely was handing out bags filled with treats for us to take home. The loudspeaker crackled, and the announcement tone sounded.

"Good afternoon," Mrs. Jenkins said over the static. "Before you leave for the day, I would like to wish you all a lovely spring break. Have fun, be safe, and watch for the *murderist*." Her announcement was immediately followed by the final bell. Everyone jumped up from their seats.

Murderist? My neck started to tingle again. It must be official: White Van Guy wasn't just kidnapping people. He was doing something worse—even worse than zapping them into a spaceship.

I rushed for the door.

Mrs. Greely yelled, "Don't forget to stay in your lines!"

She might have also said to have a nice break. I wasn't sure. I was already running down the hallway. We were supposed to form lines in the lobby: bus riders on the right, walkers on the left, and carpoolers in the middle. But I didn't have time for that. Not today. I had aliens and bullies and *murderists* to worry about. I ran straight out of the school, pushing my way through everyone.

"Hold up!" Frank yelled, chasing me out of the building. "Danny, hold up!"

I didn't stop. Not even to say goodbye to Nicholas, who had to line up for his bus. I knew he would understand, so I just kept running until I was clear across the parking lot. Only then did I let Frank catch up to me.

"What gives?" he asked. "Is this about the Bermuda Triangle?"

We started walking home our normal route. "Kind of, but kind of not. I don't know. Did you hear what Mrs. Jenkins said?"

"Yeah. So?"

"So we're in a lot of danger." I had so much jumbled in my head: Joey's threatening note, my dad with fresh bruises on his face, the murderist. With every step, I kept a close eye out for any sign of the white van—or of Joey. I wasn't taking any chances.

It wasn't fair. Until a few weeks ago, I'd never been scared to walk around in my own neighborhood. Now I wondered if I'd ever feel safe here again.

When we got to my block, I paused.

"I need to stop here," I said before turning the corner like I usually did. "Be careful getting home."

Then I knocked on Mrs. Albertini's door.

CHAPTER 25
COOKING UP A STORM

Mrs. Albertini seemed surprised when she opened the door. "You're here early. Is everything all right? Your face is flushed."

She had on a pink, frilly apron over one of those old-lady dresses she always wore.

"I ran part of the way. We got out early." I checked over my shoulder as I spoke. "For spring break."

"Well, don't stand out there in the cold. Come in."

Her house didn't smell half bad today—kind of like Mom's lasagna. That was a big improvement over stale cheese and bleach.

Mrs. Albertini had me follow her into the kitchen, but Scholly's cake wasn't on the table. She reached into the pantry and pulled out a new loaf still wrapped in plastic. "I wouldn't dare run out!"

She opened it and cut a thick slice for me before heading toward the oven.

"What are you doing?" I asked. Rows of aluminum pans lined her countertop next to the stove, where every burner had something cooking.

"Making dinner," she said. "Eggplant parmesan."

"I thought I smelled lasagna," I told her.

"Nope," Mrs. Albertini said, "but close." She held up a big, shiny purple thing.

"Your secret ingredient?" I asked.

"Not so secret," she said with a laugh. "This is the eggplant."

"You sure like your purple food."

She laughed again. "I suppose I do."

"But it's so early. And why are you making so much?" I asked.

"I have to start early to make enough for all those hungry mouths down at the factory."

"This is all for them?"

"Yes. I've been making dinner for the crew who has to work the Friday evening shift ever since my Gino took it over. When I was a child, my father always insisted we have dinner together on Friday as a family—to celebrate the start of the Jewish Sabbath. Of course, Mr. Albertini wasn't raised with the same traditions, but that didn't mean I couldn't share my traditions with him. He enjoyed our Friday night meal together as much as I did, so when he started working the Friday evening shift, I decided we'd still have our meal together, even if it meant Anthony and I would bring it to him. Well, it seemed silly to only have enough food for us when everyone down there was working so hard, so I'd make extra in case anyone wanted to join in." She smiled. "They always did, every last one of them. After Gino was gone, I still felt like the folks down at the factory were my family, so I kept bringing food. Been doing it for a very long time."

I watched as she pulled a steaming pan out of the oven. "How come you never told me that before?"

"You never asked," she said.

I guessed that was true. "My dad likes his Friday night dinner too. No matter what, he always has to have challah. Mr. Scholly bakes one just for us every week."

Mrs. Albertini reached into the plastic bag on the counter behind her and pulled out a challah. "Actually, he bakes two."

"Huh," I said. I had never wondered how Mr. Scholly knew how to make challah in the first place.

Maybe he'd learned years and years ago because Mrs. Albertini wanted to buy some from him.

"How is alien hunting going?" she asked. "Any luck?"

"Maybe," I told her. "You know that big storm we had last night?"

"My, that was awful," Mrs. Albertini said. "Shook the whole house."

"My friends and I—we don't think it was actually a storm. Not the kind caused by weather."

"You think the aliens had something to do with it?" All of her wrinkles pushed up toward her silver hair as her eyes widened.

I nodded.

"My goodness," she said, shaking her head. "Isn't that something?" She slid a piece of the eggplant parmesan onto a plate and put it on the table. "Give it a try." Unlike her borscht, this didn't look disgusting. I mean, it was covered with gobs of melted cheese. That alone was a good sign. But I wasn't big on purple food, so I cut a tiny piece off with my fork and tasted it. It was okay, actually. Kind of mushy and a little bit stringy.

"Better than borscht, but not quite up there with pizza?" Mrs. Albertini asked.

"Sorry," I said. "My dad really liked your soup. At least that's what my mom said. And she liked the rolled cabbage Frank and I made from your recipe."

"I'm glad it was a success."

I decided not to tell her that *success* wasn't the right word, especially since she'd given us all that help with the ingredients and the recipe. So instead, I said, "My dad's working tonight. I'm sure he'll like this too."

"Wonderful. I look forward to catching up with him this evening."

"You still stay there and eat with everyone?" I didn't mean to sound so surprised, but after what I'd heard Dad say last night, I suspected Mrs. Albertini might not want to stick around.

"Well, of course," she said. "What's the point of us all having a meal together if we're not *together?*"

"Oh. Right." I carefully moved the eggplant dish to the side and went back to eating my pound cake.

"So what happens next with the aliens?" she asked. "Channel Six said we might get another storm tomorrow. Do you think something big will happen?"

That was the part we'd never figured out at school. And I was supposed to have another piano lesson this afternoon. I was certain Mr. Schneider would have me record another message, but now I didn't think it was a good idea at all. My hand reached up to my mouth.

"That's your third or fourth yawn," Mrs. Albertini noted.

"I had trouble sleeping," I told her. "My dad came in late . . ."

"I'm a light sleeper too," she said. "Mr. Albertini would try so hard to be quiet after coming in from a long night, but I'd always wake up."

"It wasn't that. It was . . ." I stopped.

"It was what?" She sat down at the table.

"Aren't you going to make tea?" I asked.

"I can if you want. I didn't know you liked tea." The wrinkles on her forehead pushed together, forming even more creases than she'd had before.

"I don't," I told her.

"Oh." She relaxed her face, and all the new creases magically disappeared. "Why don't you just tell me what's on your mind?"

"My dad came home with another bruise," I said.

Mrs. Albertini sighed. "I had hoped that would have settled down by now."

"He doesn't know I know. I was supposed to

already be asleep when he got home, but I wasn't. I saw him holding ice to his face from the top of the stairs. And I heard him talking with my mom. He was pretty upset."

"I can imagine," Mrs. Albertini asked.

I turned to stare out the window to her backyard. There was an old tire hanging from a rope off a tree, kind of like the one in the park that Frank and I sometimes went to. Next to it was a crooked metal slide. I pictured Anthony with his friends out there when they were my age—back when the slide was all shiny and new. They were laughing and knocking around, and his friends didn't have to sneak into the backyard 'cause they weren't allowed to play with the Jewish boy.

"He said he wouldn't be in this mess if it wasn't for your help." I didn't turn back to face Mrs. Albertini. I just kept gazing out of the window, thinking about Anthony Albertini and his backyard friends.

CHAPTER 26
EXPLANATIONS

Mrs. Albertini didn't say anything. And I still didn't turn to face her. Not until she put her hand on top of mine. It felt like boney sandpaper, which totally freaked me out. I yanked my arm away.

"I'm sorry," she said. She kept her arm stretched across the table—I guess in case I decided I wanted to hold her hand. I didn't. I wanted her to get up and make tea or cook purple food or eat cake or anything else. "I thought I was doing the right thing," she continued.

"Did you make them give my dad a promotion?" I asked. It had been in the back of my mind ever since last night.

She looked as if she'd been waiting for me to ask this question for a million years. "He's a hard worker, your father," she said. "According to my Gino, he was one of the best. He deserved that promotion and should've gotten it a long time ago."

"But he didn't. Did you make them give it to him?" I asked again. "You still know people down there. You bring them food and stuff. They're your friends, right?" I tried not to be angry, but I could feel my voice getting louder with every word.

Mrs. Albertini's eyes met mine. The wrinkles around her mouth weren't pointing toward her ears the way they usually did when she spoke to me. Instead, they drooped down toward her chin, making her frown look way sadder than a normal frown.

"I didn't make anyone do anything," she answered. "But I did mention your father to some of the people I know in upper management."

"So it wasn't the tables?"

"I don't know anything about tables," she said. "I just know he's a good hardworking man. They were holding him back for the wrong reasons. We both know that. And I wanted them to see that." Her voice had its familiar kindness but also sounded sad.

"So that's why he got a promotion when no one else did? Because of you?"

"I thought they would wait until they had a full

group of promotions to announce," she said. "That's how they always do it. I didn't realize they would single him out and do it now. It wouldn't have been such a big deal if they'd waited."

"But it was a big deal."

"I realized that when you told me about his injury," she said. "That's why I went back to talk to some of the folks down there, but I'm afraid I made it worse. I'm sorry, Danny," she added. "I thought I was doing the right thing. It's what Mr. Albertini had wanted. I didn't know it would make things so much harder for your family."

I shook my head to keep my tears away. "You knew," I said quietly.

"No, Danny. I really didn't."

"But you knew what it was like to be the only Jewish kid in your school. You told me so. All that stuff about how the kids said awful things and how your dad was glad you weren't a boy 'cause it would've been worse." I didn't want to raise my voice, but it was the only way to keep the tears from coming. "You said the words were bad enough, and you even had a friend who had to sneak around, just like I do."

Mrs. Albertini reached for me again, but I pushed my chair back and stood up.

"Nobody here in Croyfield knows Lillian Gerstein," I continued. "They know Lola Albertini. And you named your son Anthony. Was it so nobody would guess he was half Jewish?"

Mrs. Albertini didn't answer.

"You wanted everything to be easier for him. That's what you said. You said *you knew!*"

"I made mistakes," Mrs. Albertini said, nodding. "But just because things have been a certain way for years doesn't mean they're right. I wanted to speak up for a change. We can't go on hiding forever."

"You hid the truth to help your family," I said. "You didn't take any risks with them. But what about *my* family? Everything was fine before my dad got promoted. Nobody was beating him up, and I wasn't getting bullied at school, and Nicholas didn't have to lie just to hang out with me. None of that happened before!"

"Listen to me," said Mrs. Albertini in a surprisingly fierce voice. "Your father deserved to be promoted. And he deserves to be treated better. Your entire family does!"

I'd never heard Mrs. Albertini sound angry before. I backed up slightly.

"I'm sorry," she said softly. "But if no one ever

asks for more, if no one ever takes a stand, nothing will ever change."

"They don't want us here. You're not going to change that," I told her.

"Not overnight, no," she agreed. "But small changes can gradually lead to bigger changes. We have to start somewhere."

I shook my head. "My dad's promotion isn't helping to change anything. The bosses only gave it to him as a favor to you. But it wasn't even a real favor 'cause they keep letting him know they're mad about it."

"It is making a difference," Mrs. Albertini said. "It will make things easier for others in the future. We have to keep fighting for our rights. When you stop fighting, you have nothing to gain."

"I *already* have nothing to gain!" I yelled. "That big jerk at school is never gonna quit bothering me, the people at the factory are never gonna leave Dad alone, and Nicholas's mom is never gonna let him hang out at my house. Why don't you get it? That promotion ruined everything!"

I grabbed my book bag from where I had dropped it and headed toward the living room.

"Danny, wait!" Mrs. Albertini's chair scraped

across the kitchen floor, and I knew she had stood up to follow me. "I know this has been hard for you. But we can't give up on doing what we believe in or fighting for what we deserve!"

I wanted to believe her, but twice this week my dad needed to put bags of frozen vegetables on his face because of stuff that happened at work that had nothing to do with walls. We'd tried to fight, and now everything was horrible. I ran out of Mrs. Albertini's house without even saying goodbye.

CHAPTER 27
WHITE VAN INVASION

I wanted to run home, but I ran toward Frank's house instead. Nothing felt right anymore. Mrs. Albertini hadn't even made tea, and she always made tea. She probably hated me for yelling at her when she'd only been trying to help. Plus, every time I started thinking about this Bermuda Triangle business and Mr. Schneider coming over later, my stomach twisted into a million knots.

Everything was a mess. That much I knew. I had to talk to Frank.

I sprinted down the sidewalk, around the corner, and across the street. Then I ran down two more blocks, the whole time checking over each shoulder—my right side for the white van werewolf aliens and my left for Joey Simone, who'd made it clear he was out to get me. The wind whipped across my cheeks. Mrs. Jenkins's words echoed in my ears: *"Watch for the murderist."*

I dashed halfway down another block, then up three steps toward the familiar bright yellow door. It was the only door on the street that was yellow. All the others were either green or blue.

"Frank!" I yelled, pounding my fist against the door. "Frank! Let me in!"

He swung it open and stood there with his jacket on. "What are you doing here?" he asked.

"Where are you going?" I pushed my way past him and charged into his living room, looking up and down the street through his window. When I turned around, I noticed Nicholas was standing there too. "What's going on?"

"We were just heading to your house," Nicholas said. "I had my mom drop me off here so she wouldn't know. Don't you have your piano lesson? We need to set up in your backyard."

"I'm not going to my piano lesson." The words came out choppy as I tried to catch my breath.

"Why not?" Frank asked. "If we have two tapes, the cops will have to believe us. Especially if another storm comes through when we play it.

That money is ours. And we'll be famous."

I shook my head. "He's after me," I told him.

"Mr. Schneider?" Nicholas asked. "We've already been over this. He's not going to mess with you. You're the setup."

"The what?" I peeked out the window again.

"The setup," he repeated proudly. "I saw it on TV last night after I got home. My mom went out to play bridge, and my dad let me watch his police show that I'm not supposed to watch. Anyway, there's always a setup—a guy who's the link between the big boss and the guy doing the dirty work. Someone no one suspects. That's how the bad guys get away with stuff, 'cause the cops get thrown off the trail."

"Wouldn't a setup be someone they're *setting up* to get caught?" Frank asked.

If that was true and I *was* the setup, I was in more danger than I'd thought.

"Well, never mind that part," Nicholas said. "My point is that on these shows, the bad guys always get caught in the end 'cause they make mistakes. Mr. Schneider doesn't know you're on to him. That's his mistake."

"No," I said, shaking my head again. "I'm positive

he knows. And he's planning on taking me next now that the kid from Mayson is dead."

"Dead?" Frank and Nicholas said at the same time.

"How do you know he's dead?" Frank asked.

"They stopped talking about him on the news," I explained. "I realized it earlier. Haven't you noticed?"

Nicholas and Frank both scrunched up their eyebrows the way Mrs. Greely did whenever anyone asked her a question she had to really think about.

"Yeah," Nicholas said. "Now that you mention it, I don't think I have heard anything about him lately."

"It's 'cause he's dead," I repeated. "No point in asking the public for help finding him anymore."

I was going to add that even Mrs. Jenkins knew about it, since she'd told us to watch out for his killer, when—

BOOM!

The loudest sound I'd ever heard came from outside. It was so loud the windows in Frank's house rattled. A framed family photo on the wall next to the stairs fell to the floor. Glass shattered everywhere. I wanted to run, but my feet wouldn't move, and for some weird reason, Mom's collector plates popped in my head—especially the 1976 bicentennial plate that she loved the most.

"What was that?" Nicholas cried. He swung the front door open.

"Danny!" Frank yelled, pulling on my arm to get me to follow Nicholas outside. "Come on!"

I saw the smoke far beyond the row of homes across the street, and then I felt the ground shake again.

"They've landed," I whispered. Except it was more of a terrified squeal. Sure, Mr. Schneider and his white van had freaked me out, but it still wasn't the same as a complete alien invasion.

We were in big trouble! Forget about the fancy plates—what about my family? My mom was down at the hospital, my dad was in the factory, and Alice was stuck home alone 'cause she'd been grounded. And what about Mrs. Albertini? She was alone too—probably in her kitchen cooking purple food and feeling bad 'cause I had yelled at her.

"What do we do?" Frank spun around in a panic as neighbors started to rush out of their houses. "We don't know how many Martians there are or what they want or what powers they have!"

Three police cars sped by with their lights and sirens on full blast. I took a step back from the curb. "We have to warn them!" I cried. "They have no idea what they're headed into."

I ran back into Frank's house and dialed 9-1-1 on the phone in his kitchen. A busy signal? *Crud.* I hung up.

Frank and Nicholas were still outside, talking to Frank's neighbor. It would take forever for us to warn people just by word of mouth. I picked up the receiver and tried again. After the fifth try, a woman answered.

"Nine-one-one. Please hold."

Hold? What kind of 9-1-1 service was this? I counted Mississippis in my head. Just as I got to 57, the voice came back.

"What's your emergency?" she asked.

"Alien invasion in Croyfield!" I yelled.

The woman snorted and hung up on me. I ran back outside.

"The lady at the police station wouldn't listen," I told Frank and Nicholas. "It's up to us. Do you have anything we can use as weapons?"

"No," Frank replied. "It's—"

"No, you don't have anything we can use as weapons, or no, you're not coming with me to fight them? Because I'm not going to just stand here and do nothing!"

"Stop interrupting and listen to me!" he shouted.

"There's no UFO invasion. It was an explosion. At the factory. Probably from a bunch of chemicals. My neighbor Mrs. Scavo just told me." He pointed to the cloud of smoke. "See? That's where it's coming from."

"An explosion?" I hollered. "That's even worse!" Getting attacked by aliens ranked pretty high up there on the list of awful things, but our three dads were all in the factory. Mom had always said those chemicals Dad used scared her. She'd said it plenty of times when she thought I wasn't listening.

I started to run. "Let's go!"

"Danny, wait for us!" Nicholas yelled.

Frank and Nicholas ran next to me. There were so many people out on the sidewalk that it was hard to get through, but we just kept running. We had to get to the factory.

We ran for what felt like forever, but when we reached the corner of Highland Avenue and Main Street, we had to slow down. There were too many cars moving too fast for us to run across the intersection at full speed. We wove through the traffic and started to run again when we got to the other side.

Behind us, a car honked. It was probably trying to get through too. I didn't blame it; just about everyone in this town had family working at the factory. *Everyone.*

The car honked again. And again. It sounded as if it was driving along next to us at the exact same pace that we were going. So I turned my head, and it pulled over. Then the three of us stopped in our tracks.

My brain was yelling at me to keep running. But we didn't. We just stood and watched as the side door to the white van slid open.

CHAPTER 28
WEST END MEDICAL SUPPLIES

"Get in," Mr. Schneider ordered from the driver's seat.

The ground shook again. Or maybe that was just me trembling. I clutched Frank's arm to keep my legs steady.

"Did you hear me?" Mr. Schneider snapped. "Let's go! I've been searching for you everywhere!"

"M-m-me? N-no. I-I can't," I stammered. "I'm on my way to the factory."

"I know." His voice sounded annoyed, like when I played *Ode to Joy* wrong, but there was more to it . . . more alien werewolf mixed in. "Why do you think I've been looking for you? Everyone's at the high school waiting for news. That's where I'm headed."

I glanced at Frank, then Nicholas, but I still didn't move. None of us did.

The cars behind the van honked their horns. I wanted to run to them—to scream that White Van Guy was trying to kidnap me and would zap me into outer space or worse. But I didn't. I just stood there.

"What are you waiting for? You're holding up traffic." This time, the voice came from the back of the van. It sounded familiar.

"Alice? No!" She was sitting in the third row of seats, so I jumped in and grabbed her arm to pull her out. She could thank me for saving her life later.

"Let go of me, loser!" she yelled. Then she yanked me so hard that I fell into the seat next to her.

"Hey, watch it, I'm sitting here," another voice I recognized said.

"Bobby?" I asked as he pushed me into the seat next to him.

He climbed over Alice and put his hand on the sliding door handle to close it. "You coming in or what?" he asked Frank and Nicholas. They stood frozen on the sidewalk.

"Get help!" I yelled to them, hoping they would run. Instead, they jumped inside the van. Bobby slammed the door shut and took his seat between Alice and me in the back row.

"We're not leaving you," Nicholas said, except he was gazing at Alice as he spoke the words.

He and Frank took the two seats in the middle row. With the five of us captured, Mr. Schneider drove off.

"We have to get out of here," I whispered across Bobby to Alice. "At the next stop light, we make a break for it." I wasn't sure if Nicholas and Frank could hear me from the middle row, but I knew they'd follow once they saw Alice, Bobby, and me do it. Especially Nicholas. I hoped there'd be enough time.

Alice rolled her eyes at me.

Then Bobby said, "What are you talking about?" He used his regular loud voice too. Didn't he know that if someone whispered to you, you always whispered back? Especially when it was a life-or-death situation.

"That guy," I said in an extra low voice, hoping this time Bobby would get the hint about whispering. I motioned to Mr. Schneider. "He's the white van kidnapper." And since I wanted Alice and Bobby to know how important this was, I added, "An alien kidnapper."

Bobby started to laugh. Not just a normal laugh

either. It was a snorting, snot-flying, gasping-for-air laugh. Mr. Schneider peered back at us through his rearview mirror. Then he turned on his radio, which was set to a station that played classical piano music. I could barely believe it. I leaned forward and tapped Frank and Nicholas on their shoulders. "He's sending another message," I told them. "To let them know he's got us."

Before they could respond, I felt a tug on my shirt pulling me back into my seat.

"Are you talking about Uncle Leo?" Bobby asked. "An alien kidnapper? That's a good one!"

Mr. Schneider took a sharp turn, and I nearly fell into Bobby's lap. He pushed me back over with a shove.

"No," I said, no longer worrying about whispering thanks to the loud music playing up front. "I'm talking about the guy driving the van. Mr. Schneider."

"So am I," said Bobby in an irritated tone. "He's Leo Schneider."

Frank and Nicholas both turned around in their seats to stare at Bobby. I did too. Was Bobby also an alien? Maybe that's why he'd been so mean to me lately. It was all part of the plan to capture me.

Although if I were an alien and I wanted to trick someone so I could capture them, I'd probably be nicer. To gain the person's trust and all—but that's just me.

I stared at Bobby's hands. Not a hair on them. No, if those aliens could figure out how to make Bobby without hairy hands, then they would've been able to figure out how to do it to Mr. Schneider too. Bobby was just mean for the same reason the other kids were being mean—'cause they didn't want Jewish kids around.

"Uncle Leo's married to my mom's sister," Bobby continued. "My aunt Dolores."

"He's married?" Frank asked.

"Does she know he's an alien?" Nicholas added.

"Don't be stupid," Bobby said.

"But he's a murderist," I told him.

Alice leaned over to me. "What are you babbling about now?"

"Don't you remember? Even you said he was part werewolf!" I reminded her.

"How could I forget," she said. "It was a joke, nerd face."

"It may have been a joke to you," I told her. "But it's actually true. What about his hairy hands?"

"Hairy hands don't mean anything," Bobby said. "Lots of people have those."

"Well, we know what he did," I told him. "Even Ms. Jenkins knows. She said so just today. *Watch out for the murderist.*"

"Wait. What?" Frank said.

"The murderist," I repeated. "The white van kidnapper. The guy who killed the kid from Mayson." I checked to make sure Mr. Schneider wasn't paying attention to us. Then I mouthed his name. "Don't you remember her announcement at the end of the day?"

"That's not what she said," Frank told me. "She said *watch out for the motorists.* You know, like cars. Traffic."

"Seriously," Alice said laughing, "you really are the biggest dork ever."

"But—but you saw the UFO," I said to Nicholas. "That first night with the telescope in my backyard, remember?"

"You mean the night you got scared by a couple of girls?" Alice laughed. "That wasn't a UFO. That was a meteor. Just a spinning, glowing space rock. My science teacher talked about it nonstop the next day. Yawn city."

I was having trouble absorbing all this. "But the storm and the lightning," I said. "It was just like in the Bermuda Triangle movie."

"So?" Alice asked. "We don't live anywhere near Bermuda. And what does a movie have to do with anything?"

"It has to do with everything. Mr. Schneider was sending a message to the UFO to start the storm the same way the aliens started the storms over the Bermuda Triangle before they captured all of those boats and planes."

Alice's entire expression froze. Then she started blinking at me. Just *blink, blink, blink*. It was worse than an eye roll. "I don't even know what to say," she said, but she kept talking anyway. "You know none of that is true, right?"

"How would you know?" I asked.

"Everyone knows," she continued. "All that stuff that happened in the ocean near Bermuda has to do with *science*. We learned about it in school last year, and trust me, there was nothing in our textbook about werewolf aliens sending messages to UFOs."

"My Uncle Leo's not a murderist," Bobby interrupted, his voice growing louder and angrier. "That's not even a real word. And only weirdos think aliens and werewolves exist. He's just a guy from Oxly who sells medical supplies and teaches piano." He pointed to a pile of boxes lining the wall of the van next to where we were seated. They were labeled *West Side Medical–Assorted.*

"That's how Mom knows him," Alice said. "He sells medical supplies to the hospital. Mom called him and asked him to drop off some extras at the high school because of the explosion. The hospital sent her over there. They're setting up the gym to treat people because the ER is packed and can only take the people who are hurt really badly."

My eyes darted from Frank to Nicholas to Bobby and finally to Alice.

"So there wasn't a UFO?" I asked. "And the storm was just a storm?" I shook my head in disbelief. "And Mr. Schneider is just a guy with hairy hands." I mumbled that last part under my breath.

"Duh," Alice said. "That's what we've been trying to tell you. Mr. Schneider isn't kidnapping us. He's bringing us to the high school as a favor for Mom. You should be thanking him."

"My mom's not going to know where we are," Frank said as if he hadn't just heard news that changed *everything*.

"She's probably at the high school already," Alice said. "Yours too, Nicholas."

Suddenly another thought occurred to me. "Wait, what about Dad?" I asked Alice.

"He's okay," she said. "Just a couple of scratches."

"You could have mentioned that earlier," I told her.

"You could have asked earlier," she replied. To Frank and Nicholas, she added, "I don't know about your fathers. Sorry."

They didn't respond. Not even Nicholas, who always responded when Alice spoke to him.

My eyes focused on the scene outside. There were cars and people everywhere. News traveled fast in Croyfield, especially when that news involved the factory. Mr. Schneider wove through traffic, taking the familiar route to the high school. Inside the van, piano music continued to play while we all sat in silence.

"Hey," Alice said after a minute, "maybe when we get to the high school, we'll see some of Mr. Schneider's friends, like vampire-ghost and zombie-mummy. Better hold on to your blood and brains. Oh, yeah, that's right, you don't have any brains."

"Very funny," I said, sitting back in my seat.

I knew I should have been relieved to know that there wasn't a UFO zapping up kids and that

Mr. Schneider was just a regular guy. Instead, I was kind of disappointed. I'd been so sure we'd figured everything out—the Bermuda Triangle, the white van kidnapping, even the mystery of why Mr. Schneider's hands were so hairy. But I didn't have time to think about any of that for too long.

CHAPTER 29
THE WOUNDED

We arrived at the high school, and Mr. Schneider let us out of the van. Then he jumped inside and handed each of us a box of medical supplies to carry. He glared at me before giving me a box from a separate pile behind the passenger seat. It was super heavy, and I wondered if he'd overheard some of the stuff I'd said about him.

"Let's go, Daniel!" Mr. Schneider ordered as I staggered under the weight of the box and struggled to keep up with the rest of them.

Inside the high school, a few police officers were trying to direct about a million people: injured and medical staff to the gym, family and anyone else needing information to the cafeteria. Nobody really seemed to be listening.

"Follow me!" Alice yelled above the noise. She pushed her way through the crowd, leading us down one hallway and another until we finally reached a quiet room with music stands tossed everywhere.

"We're supposed to be in the gym," I told her.

"Relax," Alice said. "I know this school. The music room is connected to the stage, and the stage is behind the gym." She headed across the room to a back door that, sure enough, opened up behind a darkened stage. Even without Alice leading, all I had to do was follow the sound of voices to know where I was headed. They grew louder with every step. When Alice finally swung open the door to the gym, I gasped.

No wonder Mom had asked Mr. Schneider to bring extra medical supplies. The place was like a scene out of that war show that Dad watched—when they bring all the injured soldiers to this one giant room to get treated. Only this wasn't a war, and these weren't soldiers.

"Frank! Over here, Frank!"

"Mom!" Frank shouted, piling his box on top of mine. They both slipped out of my hands and crashed onto my feet. I yelled a word I definitely was not allowed to say. Nobody seemed to notice.

Frank's mom rushed over and pulled him into a hug. "Thank goodness. I've been calling the house, but no one answered. I was so worried."

"Danny's piano teacher gave us a ride here," he said. "Where's Dad? Is he okay?"

"Yes, yes, he's fine. He was off-site at a meeting when the explosion hit. He's in the cafeteria now with your brother, trying to answer questions and help the volunteers get organized." She noticed Mr. Schneider and the boxes we were all carrying. "Thank you for bringing the children," she told him. "Are those the supplies Barb wanted?" She grabbed the heavier of the two boxes on the ground. "Just in time. Come on."

We followed her as she headed back through the crowd to the other side of the room. That's when I spotted Mom and Dad.

"There you are!" Mom cried, hugging Alice and me.

Dad sat in a folding chair next to her. His face had a bunch of scratches, and his arm was in a sling.

"Are you okay?" I asked.

He nodded. "The explosion pulled me right off of my feet and threw me into a wall. A real wall." He smirked, and it was kind of cool. Not 'cause he was hurt. That part wasn't cool at all. But 'cause he knew I could handle the truth. "I'm banged up a little, but nothing major."

"I'm glad you're okay," I told him. "What caused the explosions?"

"The machines in Building Two jammed up. Then the auto shutoffs malfunctioned, which meant that the chemicals and heat built up to dangerous levels. It was too much for the equipment to handle, so—*KABOOM!*" He threw his good arm up in the air. "First time in the history of the factory something like that's ever happened. I was in Building Three."

"Thank God," Mom said, knocking the tray of medical supplies in front of her with her fist three times. "All the people in here are lucky to be alive." She reached over to open the boxes Mr. Schneider lined up. "Leo, thanks so much for bringing the kids—and these supplies. We're really running low here."

"Of course," he said, searching the room. He seemed worried and, for the first time, *human*. "Bobby, I see your father and mother over there. Come on."

"Mr. Schneider?" I touched his arm as he started to walk away.

He stopped and turned to face me. "Yes, Daniel?"

"Thanks," I said. "I mean, I know my mom just said the same thing. But . . . you know." I stopped, hoping he did actually know without me having to talk to him too much longer. His super-hairy hands and buggy eyes still totally creeped me out.

"You're welcome," he replied. "I'll see you next Friday. Make sure you practice."

"Okay." I looked at Bobby, not sure what to say to him.

"Come on," Mr. Schneider urged him.

"Hey, Bobby," I called as he turned to leave. "Glad your parents are okay."

He did a squiggly thing with his lips, which I think was almost a smile or something that meant maybe he didn't hate me so much anymore. He and Mr. Schneider walked away.

Frank's mom gave him another hug. "Let's go over and see if we can help out in the cafeteria."

He waved goodbye, and they both disappeared into the crowd.

"What about my dad?" Nicholas asked. He stood on his tiptoes to scan the room. "Have you seen my dad?"

"Not yet," Mom responded, "but try not to worry. There are so many people here. He could be anywhere, or he might still be on his way over. Or he could be home."

"Or he could be somewhere else," Nicholas mumbled.

I knew what he was thinking. Alice had said some of the people were brought to the hospital. The ones who were hurt really badly . . . or worse.

"Hey," Alice said to him. "Help me unload these boxes. Then we'll go try to find him."

Nicholas took another glance around the room, and then he reached into a box to pull out a pile of bandages. He didn't even seem to notice that Alice had just spoken to him—and that it wasn't to insult him either. She was actually being nice. Plus, she was standing next to him, and her hands were in the same box as his. *They were seriously almost touching.*

"Are you okay, son? Can I help you?"

At first, I thought Mom was talking to Nicholas, but then a familiar voice responded, "I can't find my father, Joseph Simone."

My neck started to get that sweaty, prickly feeling I'd had in Mrs. Greely's class right before I went to the nurse. I spun around to see Joey standing there,

and all I could think about was his note: *you're next,*
you're next, you're next.

"Joseph Simone," Mom repeated to Dad. "Do
you know where he is?"

"Yes, they took him to the hospital," Dad replied,
his voice sounding sad.

Joey buried his hands in his pants pockets—the
same hands that had shoved me into a wall, smashed
my clay head, and formed the fist that went with that
awful note he'd written.

"Is he hurt bad?" Joey asked my mom. He didn't
look at me at all. It was like I wasn't even there, and
I wondered if he even realized he was standing next
to me.

Mom did that thing with her lips where she was
trying to smile, but it wasn't quite working. "I don't
know. But they'll take good care of him, I promise.
Are you here with anyone?"

He shook his head.

"Try not to worry." Mom put her arm around
his shoulders. "I'll see if I can find someone to drive
you over in a little bit. You can stay with us for now,
okay? You know my son, Danny, right?"

He nodded, and the sweat on my neck dripped
down into the back of my shirt.

I wasn't sure if I should say something to him, 'cause I kind of felt bad about his dad and all, but I was also scared he was still out to get me. Before I could decide, a piercing scream echoed through the gym.

CHAPTER 30
BACKYARD BOYS

Nicholas was the first one to run toward the scream. Mom ran too. I stayed back but could see that the shrieking was coming from Nicholas's mom.

"Help us, please!" she cried, holding Nicholas's dad around the waist while he limped toward us. "My husband is injured! Somebody! Please!"

His face was covered in blood. If I didn't already know the truth, I might actually think werewolf aliens had attacked him. That's how much blood there was.

Mom helped him back over to us and into an empty chair. She pressed a cloth to his head and held it there.

"He was walking out of Building Two when the explosion hit," Nicholas's mom explained. "It's a miracle he wasn't buried under the rubble."

Mom knocked three times. I knew she would. Then she said, "He needs stitches." She reached into the tray of supplies on the cart next to her.

"No," Nicholas's mom said, grasping Mom's arm to stop her. "Isn't there someone else who can do it?"

Nicholas's dad moaned. Mom pulled her arm back and gave him some water to sip. Then she started to clean his cut.

"He needs care now. He's losing blood," Mom calmly told Nicholas's mother. "A doctor will be by, but I don't know how long that could take."

Nicholas's mother scanned the jammed-packed room. Tears filled her eyes. "Are you sure there's no one else?"

Mom pulled a second chair over for her. "I've been an emergency room nurse for over twenty years and have stitched up thousands of patients. Everything will be fine."

Nicholas's mom sighed. "Okay," she said. "I'm sorry."

"I understand," Mom told her. "This is frightening for all of us. Danny," she added, "why don't you take the kids to the cafeteria? Maybe you can help out over there."

I was just about to leave when Nicholas's mom reached for my arm. "I'm sorry," she said. "I'm grateful, truly."

Mom nodded. "Go ahead," she said to me with the needle and thread in her hand.

She didn't have to ask me a third time. Seeing all that blood was making me queasy. Nicholas looked a little green too. But he also seemed relieved. When I got to the hallway, I noticed that Alice hadn't come with us, but Joey had. He kept his eyes on the ground but stayed with us as we headed into the cafeteria.

There were even more people in there than in the gym. Some were packed into lines, waiting for a turn to talk to the people with clipboards. Some were standing around talking, some were crying, and some were just sitting at the tables with glazed-over expressions. Frank and his family stood in the far corner with a person I didn't recognize.

I started to make my way toward them but stopped when Joey tapped my shoulder.

"Is your mom really gonna fix up all those people?" he asked.

Those were the first words Joey Simone had spoken to me since he told me not to leave my stuff so close to the edge of the table in art class. Unless you counted the *you're next* note he wrote. Maybe he was wondering if my mom could save me after he tried to kill me.

"She's pretty good," I replied.

He looked up at the ceiling. "And the other people at the hospital are good too? The docs and the nurses?"

"Yeah, sure," I said.

"She seems really nice. Your mom, I mean. The way she's helping all those people."

"It's kind of her job."

"But some of those people in there . . ." He paused, then went on, "I wouldn't think she'd wanna help them. After the way they . . . you know."

I shrugged. "My mom says none of that matters when someone needs help."

"Good thing," Nicholas said, "because she's fixing up my dad right now. And if your dad was here, she'd fix him up too."

Joey nodded. Then he mumbled something I couldn't hear.

Nicholas asked, "What? What did you just say?"

Joey shoved his hands in his pockets again and kept looking at the ceiling. I looked up too in case there was something actually interesting up there. Sometimes, in the cafeteria at our school, we'd throw pencils like arrows, and they'd get stuck hanging there for days until a janitor pulled them out.

"Sorry I smashed your art project," Joey said a little more clearly. "And you know, that other stuff at school. I messed up."

"Oh," I said.

"My dad was saying stuff 'cause he was mad at your dad, so I said it too. I didn't really mean . . ." His eyes met mine for a split second. "I'm just sorry."

"Yeah, okay," I told him, because he actually did sound sorry. I tried to think of something else to say, but one of the clipboard-carrying women pushed through the crowd to get to us.

"Do you boys need help?" she asked. She nervously started flipping through her pages before she even knew what we were about to say to her. "Are you trying to find someone?"

"No," I told her. "My mom's a nurse. She's in the gym right now. She sent us over to see if you needed help here."

"Oh." She did one of those smile-sigh things Mrs. Greely always did whenever someone finally gave her a correct answer to a question that I guess she thought would be easy. "Yes," the lady said. "They could use some help in the kitchen. Some of our volunteers have brought food."

"Okay, sure," I told her. It seemed like an easy way to be helpful. Plus, I was hungry.

The first person I saw when I walked into the kitchen was Mrs. Albertini. She stood behind the counter next to Anthony with her pans of food that smelled like lasagna but were really made from that weird purple vegetable. For a second, I forgot about our fight. It seemed like a really long time ago, except it wasn't at all.

"Danny," she called. She said it the same exact way as two weeks ago when she was half-hanging out her window 'cause she needed help getting noodles out of the cabinet. That was the day I found out she was Jewish.

She smiled, and the wrinkles around her mouth reached up toward her ears, no longer looking sad and angry. I smiled back at her.

"What are you doing here?" I asked.

"Anthony brought me," she said. "He always brings me. For our Friday night dinner. I figured the workers could use it now more than ever." She lined up her trays of food, making room for bowls of pasta and salad and platters of garlic bread that Anthony carried over to the counter.

"Here you go, Ma," Anthony said when he'd finished setting up the meal. In one hand, he carried her cup of tea, and in the other, he carried a challah from Scholly's.

"Thank you, sweetie," she said. "Make sure Mr. Wexler gets a piece of challah, will you? He's in the gym."

"You saw my dad?" I asked.

"Of course. As soon as I arrived, I asked about him. I'm so glad he's all right."

"I'm sorry I got mad," I told her. "You were only trying to help. I shouldn't have said that stuff."

She put her free hand on top of mine, and I didn't pull it away this time. "There's no need to apologize." Then she glanced at Nicholas and Joey standing next to me. "Are these the backyard boys you've been telling me about?"

"Nicholas is," I said. "This is Joey—we go to school together. He's waiting for a ride to the hospital. His dad's there." I'd never mentioned Joey by name to Mrs. Albertini, but even if I had, I knew she'd be nice to him. She was just like that.

"Is your dad okay?" she asked him.

"Don't know," he replied, keeping his eyes focused on his shoes.

"I'm sorry," Mrs. Albertini said. "I'll keep him in my prayers."

"Thanks," he mumbled.

"Well," she said, handing Nicholas and me each a large serving spoon. "You're here to help, yes? The crowd will be heading in any moment. Nicholas, you can dish out salad. Danny, you're on pasta." Her kind eyes moved to Joey. "Why don't you take a seat? I can bring some food out to you while you wait for your ride."

Joey nodded but didn't move. Alice rushed into the kitchen.

"Here you are," she said to him. "We have news about your dad. He's okay!"

Joey looked like he might pass out right there in the tray of cheese-covered eggplant.

Mrs. Albertini knocked three times on the wood table behind us and said, "What a relief."

"Mom called the hospital to check on him," Alice said. "He's got a broken leg, but he should heal just fine."

"That's great," I said. "I mean, not the broken

leg part, but . . . you know. Hey, I'll bet he'll let you sign his cast."

"So he's going to be okay," Joey said as if he was in a trance.

"Right," Alice told him. "We're still trying to find you a ride, but that shouldn't take much longer. Anyway, I need to get back to the gym to help." She placed three plates of food on a tray to take back with her and said she'd let the people in the gym know there was food here if they were hungry.

Joey stayed standing with us even though Mrs. Albertini had told him again he could go sit down to wait.

As people wandered into the kitchen from the cafeteria and the gym, Mrs. Albertini sipped her tea, said hello to each person, and filled their plates with food. I did the same, minus the sipping tea part. A million conversations floated through the room as people passed through.

"We even felt it in Oxly. I thought we were having an earthquake."

"Did you hear Ginny is finally getting married?"

"I'll bet someone did it on purpose. There's a lot of insurance money wrapped up in that place."

"They found that boy from Mayson."

"Wait. What?" I asked as I overfilled the woman's plate with pasta. "Oh, sorry." I took a scoop out and handed her an extra napkin. "What did you say? About the boy from Mayson?"

"They found him," she said. "A runaway. He was hiding in a shed on a farm. Poor thing."

"Whoa." I turned to see if Nicholas had heard, but Joey was now standing between us.

"Do you need help?" he asked.

"Sure." I handed him another serving spoon for the other bowl of pasta. "Thanks."

"What's this backyard thing?" he asked.

I shrugged. "It's just where we hang out. Sometimes we look at the stars and stuff with Frank's telescope."

"I've never used a telescope," he said. "Maybe I could come try it sometime?"

"Yeah, okay," I told him. I placed a spoonful of pasta on the next person's plate. "Hey, have you ever heard of the Bermuda Triangle?"

"Aliens caused it, right?" he asked.

"Yeah," I said. "That's what I think too."

MRS. ALBERTINI'S ROLLED CABBAGE RECIPE

Ingredients

1 cabbage, put in plastic bag in freezer overnight
1 pound ground turkey or low-fat meat
1 egg
¼ cup cooked rice
½ teaspoon salt
½ teaspoon pepper
1 large onion, sliced
1 28-ounce can tomato puree
1 15-ounce can tomato sauce
2 tablespoons brown sugar
1 lemon, sliced and juiced

Instructions

1. Thaw cabbage until soft, and separate leaves.

2. Mix meat, egg, rice, salt, and pepper. Set aside.

3. In a large pot, combine onion, scraps from cabbage, tomato puree, and tomato sauce. Bring to a boil.

4. Spoon meat and rice mixture into each cabbage leaf, roll, and fold securely at each end.

5. Place the rolls into the pot. Sprinkle with brown sugar to taste. Add lemon juice and cut-up lemon slices.

6. Cook on low heat for 1 hour.

7. Transfer to the baking tray and put into a 350-degree oven for an additional hour before serving.

ACKNOWLEDGMENTS

One evening in the 1970s, my mother and I looked out the living room windows as a mysterious oval object surrounded with lights hovered above us in the sky. I thought for sure we'd seen a UFO. It turned out to be the Goodyear Blimp. By the time I found out the truth, it was too late. The "what-ifs" had already entered my mind. While *The Backyard Secrets of Danny Wexler* is a work of fiction, many of the scenes and snippets of conversations were pulled directly from my own childhood—including my possible UFO sighting, the factory that exploded several miles away and shook my house, and the one memorable Friday before spring break when my elementary school principal, whom I adored and trusted, did indeed say, "Watch out for the motorists," even though my second-grade ears heard "Watch out for the murderist." There were also moments of anti-Semitism and bullying, both in school and out. I grew up in a town with a strong Jewish community, but we were not immune.

These memories provided an abundance of inspiration. However, this book would not exist without the endless support of many friends, family, colleagues, and early readers.

To my "Weggie Writers"—Donna Galanti, Tori Bond, Janice Bashman, Kathryn Craft, Kate Brandes, Linda Wisniewski, Dana Schwartz, and Lisa Papp— thank you for your wisdom, laughs, inspiration, and friendship. I am forever indebted to Donna Galanti, who one snowy day mentioned a childhood piano teacher with hairy hands. I feel compelled to mention he was *not* a white van werewolf alien kidnapper, but he did weave his way into my imagination.

To Sarah Clayville, my trusted critique partner and good friend, I would be truly lost without your critical eyes, remarkable talent, and kind soul. You've been with Danny's story from start to finish, and I can't thank you enough for the countless times you've read through chapter revisions, each time with enthusiasm and integrity. I'm so grateful.

I'm also truly blessed to have the world's greatest

cheerleaders in my three children, Joshua, Sarah, and Cole. My heart overflows with love for you. Thank you also to my parents and other wonderful family, whom I love so much. Thanks to my grandmother, who I'm sure would be filled with joy to know her rolled cabbage recipe inspired part of the story. And to Tim, thank you for reminding me to find happiness every day.

This book certainly would not be here without the help and encouragement of my agent, Barbara Krasner, and the team at Kar-Ben and Lerner Publishing. I'm also so appreciative to the early readers, both young and grown, at PJ Library and PJ Our Way for their invaluable feedback and desire to help my story come to life.

Finally, thank you, readers, for allowing me to share my story with you. While the book takes place in the past, anti-Semitism is still very much a part of our present. Together, we can make a difference.